Delaney's Sunrise

Rhonda Lee Carver

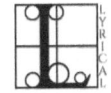

LYRICAL PRESS
Kensington Publishing Corp.
www.kensingtonbooks.com

Lyrical Press books are published by
Kensington Publishing Corp. 119 West 40th Street New York, NY 10018

All Kensington titles, imprints, and distributed lines are available at special quantity discounts for bulk purchases for sales promotion, premiums, fund-raising, and educational or institutional use.

Special book excerpts or customized printings can also be created to fit specific needs. For details, write or phone the office of the Kensington Special Sales Manager:
Kensington Publishing Corp.
119 West 40th Street
New York, NY 10018
Attn. Special Sales Department. Phone: 1-800-221-2647.

Kensington and the K logo Reg. U.S. Pat. & TM Off.
Lyrical Press and the L logo are trademarks of Kensington Publishing Corp.

First Electronic Edition: June 2011
eISBN-13: 978-1-61650-283-6
eISBN-10: 1-61650-283-5

First Print Edition: June 2011
ISBN-13:]978-1-61650-859-3
ISBN-10: 1-61650-859-0

Printed in the United States of America

Five years ago, Dee Crawford's engagement to Jacob Delaney ended in death.

Jacob's secrets followed him to his grave–and chased Dee from Delaney's Farm, and from his brother Abe's forbidden embrace. Yet when her own secrets send her back to Ohio and right into Abe Delaney's arms, old guilt comes to light, old passions reignite, and Jacob's secrets return to haunt them with more than just his memory. Someone in town wants Dee gone, and will do anything to stop her from uncovering the truth about her fiance's death. If Dee is to survive, she must expose Jacob's long-buried secrets…and expose her heart to Abe. Only by admitting their love can they ease the guilt that has plagued them for years. But will love be enough to save Dee when the next death on Delaney's Farm may be her own?

Books by Rhonda Lee Carver

Dreaming Ivy
Castle's Fortress
Friends with Benefits
With Honor

Published by Kensington Publishing Corporation

To Jay

Acknowledgements

To my children. Thank you to Tharp Animal Health Center who graciously answered questions. To all of the farmers in Ohio. To Todd for listening and car chases. To my readers...may you always find a smile

Chapter 1

Dee Crawford switched off the radio as she passed the road sign. *Willow Creek, One Mile Ahead.*

Anticipation and apprehension slithered up her spine like chilly fingers. Beads of sweat broke out on her forehead and between her breasts, so she rolled down the window of her Jeep. The brisk breeze cooled her feverish skin, but did little to diminish her uneasiness.

Taking a much-needed breath, slow and measured, Dee counted to ten, one of many relaxation techniques she'd absorbed from motivational CDs on the long drive from Chicago to Ohio's farmland. She'd need every last trick to manage her rolling stomach. She'd stopped at a greasy diner two hundred miles back and packed away more than a thousand calories worth of cheeseburger, fries, and strawberry milkshake. She hadn't had a good burger in at least five years--not since she moved away. Thinking back, she couldn't believe she'd once attempted a diet of tofu, bean sprouts, and eggplant.

More than once friends had called her crazy for her impulsiveness, yet Dee considered herself fairly level-headed. On the other hand, coming back to Willow Creek was probably downright nuts. Since she'd decided to return to the small-town home she'd hastily abandoned, she'd questioned her sanity repeatedly.

Past experience told her nothing but trouble waited in Willow Creek.

Dee pushed her thoughts into the back of her mind and kept her attention on the road.

A few miles later, she passed a familiar run-down barn and on the next curve, Dee turned onto the bumpy country road. For the next five minutes, she dodged cracks and potholes until she finally passed under the large *Delaney's Farm* sign.

One dark, dreary night, she'd pulled out of this very road and bid farewell to country living and everything that went with it. At the time, she'd thought leaving was the only way to rid her life of the guilt and sadness that had filled her.

And the only way to forget Abe Delaney.

Dee studied the scenery as she drove along the narrow gravel drive. She slowed the Jeep as she passed layers of thick, lush pine trees as green as if a painter had painted them that very moment. She breathed in the tangy, fresh scent. A tingle of awareness swirled in her chest. She'd yet to find a sweeter smell.

Dee glanced past the line of foliage to the sweeping view of the large pond. Ducks floated by an old gray fishing boat. A fishing rod stood propped against the hull.

She drove past red barns. The smells of hay and cow dung wafted on the breeze. A city girl's worst nightmare--or maybe not. Better than car exhaust fumes. Spotting a regal stallion trotting along the white fence, Dee smiled. One didn't see that in the city.

Reaching the north side of the property, she gazed across the blueberry grove and, beyond that, a section of green pasture. "Beautiful," she said aloud.

The solitude and peace of the landscape comforted her. She could feel her blood pressure drop and her anxiety float away.

The large white farmhouse hadn't changed a bit from what she remembered. It was still lovely enough to be featured on the front cover of *Country Home Magazine.* Large windows were framed in pristine curtains. The traditional wraparound porch was lined with rockers, welcoming someone to sit with a glass of iced tea as the evening passed.

Delaney's Farm was the most pleasant, dreamy place she'd ever seen. Built in the 1800s, it had started out as the town's first school. In those days, it was a one-room structure. Soon after the Delaney family bought it, they built on rooms and turned it into a comfortable home.

Dee parked, turned off the Jeep's engine, but didn't make a move to get out. She scanned the front of the house, looking for any sign of life. Not that she'd expected a red carpet welcome, but simple acknowledgement of her arrival would have been nice.

Abe had driven her away five years ago, and his sentiments probably hadn't changed. She had written to tell him she was arriving, but he hadn't responded. She hadn't been surprised. When his brother, Jacob, had died in a tragic car accident two weeks before he'd planned to marry Dee, life had taken a severe turn for the worse.

Closing her eyes and taking a deep breath, she finally slid out of the driver's seat, stretching her tired muscles. The sun beat down on her skin, and she glanced at the bright blue sky. It was an unusually hot day for May in Ohio, and she expected it to get much hotter once she came face to face with Abe.

Dee removed her bags and dropped the three leather cases to the gravel, studying them with disappointment. It was somewhat debasing to realize everything she owned sat before her.

But this was her chance for a new beginning. It was time she made a change. Would Abe realize that?

Dee heard the squeak of the screen door opening. Her heart beat faster. She turned, expecting to find a tall man sporting a frown. Instead, she came eye to eye with a silver-haired woman wearing an apron. Dee dropped her gaze to the woman's hands, which clasped tightly against her large bosom. From the older woman's narrowed eyes and glower, Dee wasn't a welcome sight.

Planting a winning smile on her face, Dee stepped up on the porch and offered her hand. "Hello, I'm Dee Crawford."

"Yes, Ms. Crawford," the other woman replied with a curt nod. "We've been expecting you."

Dee pulled back her hand and hooked her thumb in the front pocket of her jeans. "Please call me Dee. I'm glad Abe received my letter. I'm sorry, but he didn't reply, so that kind of puts me at a disadvantage."

With a pensive look and a sideways tilt of her head, the woman said, "I'm Mrs. Graves. I've been the housekeeper here at the farm for four years. I do the cleaning and the cooking."

The woman's attitude grated, but Dee took it with a grain of salt. Mrs. Graves could have waited to find a reason to dislike her before jumping to conclusions. Dee didn't intend to step on any toes.

"Thanks for greeting me, Mrs. Graves."

"Abe asked me to show you in if you showed up."

She sucked in a breath and bit her bottom lip as she swallowed her trepidation. Retrieving her bags, Dee made her way back up the steps to the porch. Mrs. Graves stepped to the side and held the door open. As Dee passed, she lost her grip on the luggage. One bag slid down her arm, falling to the wooden floor with a loud *thump*.

Mrs. Graves's mouth thinned as she examined the floor, as if looking for damage. "Do you need any help?"

Dee looked at the woman. Was she serious? Biting back laughter, Dee shrugged. She turned her attention to the familiar decorations of the foyer. Framed pictures of family still filled one wall, and she glanced over generations of Delaneys with their coal-black hair, dazzling smiles, mocha eyes, and olive complexions.

Her favorite picture, positioned significantly in the middle, was surrounded by an arrangement of smaller snapshots. Five Delaneys stared back at her as she examined the family portrait taken more than twenty years ago.

Ted Delaney had a proud tilt to his chin, and his warm eyes reflected his love for his wife and three sons. Mary Delaney stood next to her husband with devotion beaming in her kind, gentle smile. Behind the couple stood three handsome sons who were very similar in looks, yet so different in lifestyle.

The middle son, Max, was also the tallest, with a square jaw, a short military buzz cut and a face set in stoic lines From what she remembered, he was a Navy Seal and didn't make it home often because of his many assignments overseas.

Abe, the eldest, had thick black hair with soft, silken waves. His deep, mysterious eyes reminded her of a warm pool of melted chocolate. The proud set of his jaw said he was a force to reckon with. She should know. She'd gone head to head with him on more than one occasion. Her blood pressure rose to scorching heights at the mere memory of their arguments. She resisted the urge to fan herself.

Her gaze settled on Jacob, the youngest, the man she'd met and intended to marry. He'd had boyish features, welcoming, friendly, and in the picture he wore a mischievous smile. Of the three brothers, he looked most like their mother. The Jacob she'd known opened his heart to everyone, but in the end his deeply-concealed secrets had destroyed his happiness.

Tears stung her eyes. She blinked them back. Five years later, and her raw emotions still stung her like needles of devastation.

The sound of rubber-soled shoes on the polished floor, followed by an intrusive cough, pulled Dee from her thoughts. She turned and offered Mrs. Graves a forced smile. "That photo always grabs my attention."

Mrs. Graves shrugged. "Can I get you anything? Lemonade? Tea? Something to eat?"

Dee shook her head. Tendrils of hair fell against her face, cooling her heated cheeks. She brushed them back. "No, thank you. I'll just get my things settled into my room."

"Abe asked me to show you into the guest room--"

"The guest room?" Dee blurted between tight lips.

Mrs. Graves's eyes narrowed into slits. "Is there a problem?"

"I planned to stay in my old bedroom." Dee didn't want to make waves, but she didn't consider herself a guest.

Several expressions flickered over the other woman's face, until indifference swept through her blue-gray eyes. "Then so be it. I can prepare the bedroom with fresh sheets."

Dee waved a hand. "No, no. I can take care of it."

With a brusque nod, Mrs. Graves turned on her heel and started out of the room. Dee caught the woman before she disappeared. "Mrs. Graves, is Abe home?"

Mrs. Graves turned. Her cool glare pierced Dee from across the room. "No. He's out."

Dee let her leave without further interruption. The older woman reminded Dee of her pinch-faced second grade teacher. Mrs. Halesworthy had worn thick-soled shoes that made swishing sounds as she walked through the halls of the school. The teacher had carried her pointing stick like a weapon. If a kid broke a rule, Mrs. Halesworthy could scare the child until they peed their pants. She didn't doubt Mrs. Graves could frighten kids, and probably most adults.

Now that she was happily alone, Dee couldn't resist checking out the first floor. She felt like a child on Christmas morning. She'd always found silent stories in the antique furniture Mother Delaney had collected from all over the country.

She felt like an intruder as she snuck a glance into the living room. The décor transported her back into the 1800s. Dark wood, polished and refined, trimmed walls papered in solid red. Years of gentle wear had softened the finish on cherry hardwood floors. The paisley brown rug centered before the fireplace was new--or at least to her. The colors complemented the beige upholstery of the couch and chair.

The built-in shelves were also new, and brimming with books. She could guess Abe had read each one, maybe twice, some three times. He was a complex man. Country living sizzled in his blood during the day, but by night he was a scholar who buried himself in books. He'd even given thought to writing his own novel.

Dee headed toward the kitchen for a drink, but decided against it when she heard the sound of clinking dishes. Mrs. Graves wouldn't appreciate her company. Instead, she lugged her bags up the staircase and down the long hall. Luggage-lifting would have made one kick-ass workout, because she was exhausted by the time she reached her bedroom. Maybe her personal trainer had been a waste of money

It didn't matter anymore. No more personal trainers, luxury gyms, gourmet coffee shops on every corner or fancy restaurants. Willow Creek was far from the city. Coming back to the quiet town, she'd given up all the lavish perks for a simpler way of life. She hadn't found a drop of happiness in Chicago.

Maybe country life would steer her toward contentment.

The closest thing she'd get to a gym in these parts was milking the cows, weeding the gardens and harvesting the crops. If she wanted gourmet coffee, she'd have to brew it herself. Fancy eating wasn't a concern, considering she'd worked as a caterer for ten years and could toss together a fine meal when the mood struck. She wasn't giving up anything in the long run, right?

She lingered in the hallway with her hand on the bedroom doorknob. Taking a calming breath, she pushed the door open and crossed the threshold.

It was still her room. Nothing had changed. The pale blue walls, the white trim, the black sleigh-style wooden headboard all remained. She'd picked out the thick white comforter and colorful pillows herself. The matching chest once held framed pictures, but she'd taken them with her. She'd have them returned by nightfall.

Apprehension knotted her stomach as memories filled her mind. She tried to nudge them away, but they burrowed deeper.

Outside she heard the crunching of tires on gravel, drawing her to the large bay window. Tossing the smallest bag onto the bed, she pulled back the sheer lace curtain, and peered out at the front yard and the twisting, narrow drive. Abe's black truck came into view, leaving a cloud of dust in its wake.

Dee watched with bated breath as Abe parked in front of the house. Seconds later, he slid out from the driver's side. The morning sun glinted off his hair, turning it almost a faint purple. Blue flannel drew attention to his broad shoulders, while worn jeans accentuated the length of his toned legs. An odd feeling washed over her. Abe lifted his head, looking directly at her. A moan escaped her lips. Her heart clenched, and butterflies flitted in her stomach. He stared up at her. His steely, dark gaze penetrated her through the window.

With a twist of her wrist, she let the curtain drop and jumped back. She brought a shaky hand to her chest and ordered her body not to betray her. She closed her eyes and forced her breathing to slow. Abe was a mere man. He had no control over her. Or did he?

It'd taken months of mental preparation, as well as exhaustive planning, for her to come back to the farm. When she had left, she'd sworn she'd never return under any circumstances. Not as long as Abe remained.

She had been engaged to Jacob for less than two days when he'd brought her to Delaney's Farm. She hadn't been ready to meet the older, tougher brother Jacob had told her about. Jacob never could have prepared her for Abe. She remembered all too well how he'd besieged her with his curious chocolate-colored eyes. They had burned a hole through her then--as they would now.

She brushed her clammy palms down her pants and fidgeted with the lace edging her top. She'd have to face Abe again, sooner or later. Time to get it over with.

Taking a seat at the vanity, she stared at her reflection in the mirror. It seemed as though the hands of time had molded her face with their cool touch. People said she was pretty. She supposed it was true, in a classic, delicate way. Her hair was a shade of light chestnut, natural--unlike her friends, who had to color theirs every three months.

Her skin was fair, and she never tanned. Her mother had told her a hundred times that wrinkles were never flattering. Her pale, freckled nose and cheeks were the legacy of her equally pale, freckled grandmother.

She puckered her lips. They were thin. Ever since she could remember, she'd wished for a supple, full pout. However, just like her breasts, her lips had never reached ample proportions.

Oh well. There was more to life than big breasts and full lips.

She did have an ample brain, at least.

With a glance down her clothes, she sighed. The pink, frilly, long-sleeved shirt, gray slacks and tall boots made her look like a professional attending an important conference. She knew Abe. He'd get a laugh out of her outfit. He would think she was foolish wearing high heels on a farm. She would stick out among the horse barns and greenery like a sore thumb.

She changed into a pair of dark denims, tight t-shirt, and boots. "Calm and collected," she repeated to herself as she emerged from the bedroom.

She found Abe in exactly the same spot where she'd met him five years ago: sitting on the front porch. He stared at the blueberry bushes as if searching for answers in the tranquil scenery. He was probably asking Mother Nature how he could get her off his land.

Some things never changed. Had Dee really believed Abe would? Men like him never changed. He made people come to him. No doubt he'd have sat there and waited until she made the first move.

Stepping through the creaky screen door, she made her way toward him. The summer heat brushed a soft breeze across her face, warming her. Sweat beaded on her upper lip, but she attributed it to frayed nerves more than the temperature. She wiped the moisture, paused and waited. He knew she was there, but made no effort to look at her.

Wasn't he the least bit curious? *Turn and look at me!*

She followed his gaze out over the blueberry grove. The cloudy sky promised rain, and a group of deer ate grass along the edge of the trees. She swept her eyes over him. His hair was longer, covering his ears and nearly touching the collar of his flannel button-down. A layer of stubble dusted his cheeks, and his jaw was set in a tight, grim line.

She silently urged him to acknowledge her. She wished he'd make this easier for them both.

He brought his hand to his mouth, sucking on the cigarette he clamped between his fingers. He inhaled and exhaled as if it were a ritual. Finally, he took one last, long drag and ground the butt out on the wooden post.

Without anything to keep him occupied, he turned and caught her with a piercing look. It shook her to the core. It was clear by his narrowed, hard eyes and the bitter scowl that he would be doing everything in his power to make her stay here a bad experience.

She wanted to turn tail and rush back into the house, to find solace in her bedroom alone, but she stood her ground. She controlled her body, refusing to quiver under his raw scrutiny, even while she turned into gelatin inside.

He was only a man. She told herself to not back down.

Holding her head high and her back straight as a rod, she endured the sweet pain as his gaze scoured every inch of her. He visually caressed her, from the roots of her hair to the very tip of her new, shiny boots. His examination was purposeful and exaggerated, as if he intended to unnerve her.

Unfortunately, he did. The strength in his menacing eyes, his high cheekbones, and large frame were enough to alarm anyone.

Time had worked its invisible hands on him, too. Lines etched the skin around his eyes and mouth, but age hadn't taken anything away from his striking good looks. Instead, he appeared more distinguished and breathtaking. She couldn't deny the attraction that drew her. He was desirable, and could be devastatingly charming when he wanted to be. He just never wanted to be.

She'd always believed Abe was born in the wrong era. He should have lived and fought with the likes of Jesse James and Doc Holliday. Seeing him sitting there with his worn, torn jeans, his old shirt and scuffed boots, one would never guess he was a man who'd once worked in a multi-billion dollar financial organization.

Dee hadn't known Abe then. But she'd heard he wore Armani suits, drove a fancy car and lived in a luxurious penthouse in Manhattan.

Their eyes met. His were icy. She reminded herself they shared common interest...and familiar pain.

"I'm glad you got my letter." Her words sounded weak, edged in fear, even to her own ears. "I didn't think it was fair to just show up without notice."

He kept his gaze steady, locking her in place with its intensity. "What the hell are you doing here?"

She swallowed, her throat dry. "Thanks for the warm welcome. I knew I could count on your hospitality."

"You didn't answer my question." His voice deepened.

Calm and sure, she ordered her nerves.

He wanted to scare her into running away. She'd given him that pleasure five years ago, but never again, even if it meant growing a thicker skin and an even thicker heart.

"Abe, do I really need to answer that question?"

One booted foot propped against the railing, and the other stretched out in front of him as if he had no concern in the world. He slowly eased himself up until he stood his full height, six foot two, and a good two-hundred pounds. She knew he didn't have an ounce of fat under his shirt and jeans. As he moved, his shirt clung to six-pack abs and toned biceps. She'd forgotten how intimidating his tall frame could be, especially compared to her five foot four, one-hundred-ten pound frame.

He crossed the short distance between them. The scuff of his boots deafened her. Rolling her head back on tight shoulders, she looked up at him, refusing to squirm no matter how heated his gaze grew. He stopped within inches, towering over her.

"You're not welcome here." His voice was a raspy whisper. His lips thinned, and one corner of his mouth dropped.

Dee brought her arms up and hugged herself protectively, placing a palm over her chest. Was her blood pumping from fear...or excitement?

Her lips trembled. She wasn't afraid of him, but panic whirled inside her. He'd always had that effect on her. She'd hoped maturity would give her the advantage in controlling her reactions. Obviously her brain was on a different track than her spiraling feelings. Five years hadn't dampened the rushing of her blood, the butterflies in her stomach or her trembling hands.

She knew all too well that underneath the harsh, brawny exterior existed a teddy bear's heart. Once upon a time, Abe had opened up to her. She'd glimpsed kindness and tenderness. If Dee had to guess, she'd say he didn't let many people see the softer side.

He'd just have to get used to the idea that she was back.

"Abe," she started, then stopped to moisten her lips. "I'm not here to cause problems. Can't we just let go of the past and start a new friendship?"

The muscles clenched in his neck. She waited for him to snap.

"Let go?" His words were laced with anger. "It may be easy for you to forget the past, Dee, but he was my brother. Dammit, Jacob was my brother!"

"And he was my fiancé."

"He was your fiancé for two months. He was my brother for twenty-six years." His hands clenched into fists, and the line of his jaw hardened.

She exhaled and tucked a tendril of hair behind her ear. The breeze picked up, carrying his scent to her nostrils. She inhaled the masculine smell. It brought back the familiar feeling of when his kisses had melted her. She moistened her bottom lip and silently swore as neglected muscles throbbed.

"This isn't a contest to see who has more of a right to mourn Jacob's death, Abe." She refused to look away. "We both loved him and lost him, and together we buried him. If we can't get along for any other reason, it should be for his memory." She rolled her next words around her mind before she continued. "He left me his share of Delaney's Farm because he wanted me here."

He laughed. "Who the hell do you think you're talking to, Dee? Last I looked, I didn't have *easily manipulated* written across my forehead." His lip curled. The explosion was coming, but she didn't back away. "Look at you, Dee." He ran his gaze over her frame. He should have just licked her from forehead to toes. It evoked the same feeling. "You don't belong here. You come here in your fancy clothes and your shiny shoes and place yourself smack dab in the middle of *my* life. You believe you belong here because my brother willed you his half of the farm? You have no rights." He turned on a booted heel and stalked to the railing, placing both hands on it. "Although Jacob owned half, he didn't have the right to give it to you."

"I offered to sign it over to you, remember? We were sitting in the attorney's office after the reading of the will and I told you I didn't want the farm. I knew it wasn't right for me to have it." Her heavy sigh seemed to slice through the tension. "You refused to let me sign my share over to you."

He gripped the wood railing until his knuckles turned white. "Are you here to make that offer again?"

Dee clasped her hands tightly. To Abe, she was just a lingering sign of Jacob's rebellion. If Jacob had willed her his half of the farm, it was--in Abe's mind--just another impulsive act in a long string of impulses that had centered around Dee. Jacob hadn't been thinking clearly, Abe had said. After Jacob's death, he'd accused her of clouding both their minds with her hypnotic poison.

He turned. His emotions seemed under control, and his triple-layered wall appeared back in place. "Are you going to answer me? Are you here to make that offer again?"

She narrowed her eyes. "No."

He pushed away from the rail and brushed past her. She kept her gaze on his back as he stomped off the porch. "That's fine," he muttered. "You'll run again. The sooner, the better."

Chapter 2

Dee watched as Abe marched toward the barn, his back stiff and his hands shoved deep into his pockets. Icy fingers of dread skimmed down her spine and the butterflies in her stomach fluttered wildly. She'd expected his anger. What she hadn't anticipated was the way her body still responded to him with such profound intensity. She should be repulsed. She wasn't.

She turned on her heel and came face-to-face with Mrs. Graves, who blocked the doorway. The woman looked like a mama bear coming to her cub's rescue. Dee could respect that Abe had a guardian, though he was the last one who needed protection. With a shrug and a fake smile, Dee said, "Well, that went well."

Mrs. Graves threw her head back and sniffed loudly. "I found it much like snake charming. The charmer hypnotizes the reptile simply by playing an instrument." Her cool gray gaze slid over Dee's body in silent implication.

Dee stiffened her spine. "Am I the charmer in that comparison?"

"You know what they say, if the scales fit..."

"Well, I can assure you, *they* never met Abe Delaney." Dee brushed past Mrs. Graves, fighting back the threatening mist of tears. She was a strong woman; she could handle the devil and his guard. She only needed a moment to regain her balance.

Back in her bedroom and safely tucked away from both Mrs. Graves' judgmental eye and Abe's harsh attitude, she finally swallowed the lump in her throat. She scrubbed her knuckles against her damp eyes with a groan.

Could the situation get any worse? She fell back onto the bed, pulled the downy blanket over her and closed her eyes.

"Okay, Jacob." Her voice echoed in the empty room. "I'm here at the farm. Your brother despises me. I suspect that Mrs. Graves, whom I've never met before today, hates me too. I'm sure you have your reasons for leaving me your share of ownership, but for the life of me I'm stumped."

After a good period of sulking, Dee moved from the bed and caught a glimpse of herself in the full-length mirror. She hadn't worn jeans in years. She found them comfortable. Her lifestyle in Chicago wasn't fitting for jeans and boots. Designer clothes and lavish embellishment had been the norm.

Who had she become since she moved to Chicago?

She was only a fragment of that naïve girl who'd met a man, a week later agreed to marry him, and flown home with him to a farm located in nine-oh-two-one-nowhere. She'd blame the impulsiveness on lust, but no, that was impossible. Their relationship hadn't gotten to that level.

She had known little about Jacob. There were things a woman needed to learn about a man before she said "yes" to the engagement. She'd gone into the relationship curious about his middle name, his favorite color, and what he slept in at night--if he slept in anything at all.

People should know those things about a partner before they promised to spend their lives together. Her mother had been right when she'd told her not to jump into marriage with a stranger.

Jacob had died before the wedding, but in truth their relationship had ended weeks before. They'd never have gone through with the ceremony. He'd destroyed a large part of her innocence. Her hopes of a happy ending had been smashed. When she'd found out Jacob had been living a double life she'd been floored. She'd had no clue who he truly was until he told her the truth.

She pulled away from the mirror. As tempting as it was, she couldn't hide in her bedroom all evening. Things wouldn't change on their own. She had the power to make things better--and hoped Abe would come around, eventually.

Feeling refreshed, she bounded downstairs. Mrs. Graves was working in the kitchen. Dee glanced across the room, admiring the modern stainless steel appliances and new cherry wood cabinetry. It was about time Abe got rid of the old stove and dated decor. This was a kitchen she could create culinary art in.

"Hello, Mrs. Graves."

Mrs. Graves glanced up from kneading dough, gave Dee a brisk nod, then continued to pound the tan blob on the counter with a wooden rolling pin.

Dee leaned against the cutter-board island, glancing across the mound of sliced apples, a variety of spices and a bowl of butter. "Those apples smell delicious."

Pausing again, Mrs. Graves brushed a loose curl off her forehead. "They're from the trees in the grove. Apple is Abe's favorite pie." A hint of a smile lifted the corner of her thin mouth, but it didn't quite reach her eyes.

How could she forget apple was Abe's favorite? She'd made him more than one pie while she lived on the farm. "Well, I'd be happy to lend a hand. Apple pie is one of my specialties." She stole a piece of apple and popped it into her mouth. The crisp, sweet and juicy fruit brought her taste buds alive as her mind conjured up an array of recipes she could create with them. Recipes to seduce a man right out of his boots. She cleared her throat--and her mind. "I bet these make great pies."

With a tired sigh, the older woman shook her head. "With all due respect, Ms. Crawford, I enjoy working alone."

A tinge of hurt tugged at her heart. She understood some people enjoyed baking because it relaxed them, but the other woman's cool attitude had nothing to do with anything so simple.

Stepping back from the countertop, Dee straightened her back and dredged up a smile. "If you change your mind, let me know. Maybe you'd share a few secrets on how you roll your dough without tearing it."

With that, Dee left her alone.

* * * *

In the barn, Abe grabbed another beer from the cooler and struck the cap against a wooden beam. The top popped off and twirled through the air, landing in the cooler with a clink. He smiled as he brought the long neck to his lips and guzzled half before settling onto his favorite makeshift seat: a bale of hay.

A cold brew never tasted better than when in his special place, which just happened to be the horse barn. He needed a buzz this evening. He could use a smoke too, but never lit up in the barn, and didn't want to venture outdoors just yet.

He cursed himself for picking up the habit again after dropping it nearly seven years ago. Another bad habit to add to the long list he'd accumulated over the last few months. He blamed Dee for almost every single one of them.

Running his fingers through his hair, he made a mental note to get a trim. His entire schedule had been screwed since Dee had said she was coming. He hadn't been able to concentrate on anything but the idea that she'd be living at the farm. He shook as he remembered his anger when he'd finished the letter.

She had no right to be here. He couldn't care less if a piece of paper stated she owned half *his* land.

No one, not even the law, could make her presence acceptable.

"You out here hidin'?"

Abe frowned as Mitch Goody, his friend and farm hand, ducked through the doorway. "I'm not hiding."

"Got your company, I see," Mitch said in his slow Texas drawl.

"Buddy, the term 'company' implies she's welcome." Abe grabbed an unopened beer from the cooler and tossed it to Mitch. "Pull up a bale. Bet you could use a cold one, too."

"I believe I'll do that." Mitch settled onto the bale.

"Are the cows looking good?" Abe asked.

After taking a long draw from the bottle, Mitch nodded. "They're working out fine on the north end." Mitch removed his black Stetson and scratched his thick mane of sandy curls. "Your unwelcome guest settling in okay?"

"Dammit!" Abe swore; Mitch jerked. Abe jabbed a thumb toward the house. "I'm a stranger in my own home." His anger, which had just begun to ebb, swelled again. "I can't even relax in my own bed."

The black stallion in the farthest stall whinnied as he dug a hoof at the ground.

"It's okay, Danger. She's too afraid of horses to come anywhere close to the barn." Abe chuckled. He was safe here.

Mitch slid him a curious glance. "Would you be sittin' around in that big ol' house right now?"

"If I wanted to, I couldn't," he said.

Mitch broke into laughter. Abe snorted. The situation wasn't the slightest bit funny. He finished off his beer. He was done for the night. He had to get up early in the morning, and the last thing he needed was a hangover on top of his troubles. His mare Sally came to the edge of her stall and neighed softly, tapping her foot. Abe laughed. "Don't you start with me too, old girl."

Mitch pushed his hat back on his head and shrugged a broad shoulder. "In my family, Abe, we stick together. Dee is your family."

Abe bit back a scowl. His idea of family wasn't a woman who weaseled her way into his property. "She's not family. She was engaged to my brother. That doesn't make her blood thicker than water, my friend."

He'd only briefly discussed Dee with Mitch. A man didn't need to air his troubles to everyone, not even good friends.

Mitch shook his head and said, "That sounded a lot like bitterness, pal. She didn't betray Jacob, did she?"

Abe narrowed his eyes. "Why do you ask that?"

Mitch shrugged. "Somethin's ruffled your feathers."

Abe leaned his back against the rough wood and thought back five years. "No, she didn't betray him," he answered softly. "But two months don't make her family." He held up two fingers. "Two. Anyway, whose side are you on?"

"Yours, partner. Or," there was a long pause, "maybe not."

Abe raised his head. "What?" He stared at Mitch, who froze with his bottle caught in midair and eyes rounded. "What's wrong with you?" Abe followed Mitch's stare to the open barn door.

Dee stood in the doorway, her fists planted on her hips, her lips pursed accusingly.

"Oh, shit," Abe whispered.

"Am I interrupting?" Dee took the first step across the threshold of his private zone.

There went *his* space.

"Hell yes." Abe shook his head. He caught Mitch ogling Dee appreciatively and wanted to clock him in the jaw. "Can't a man have a beer in peace?" he asked.

"Are you expecting an answer?"

"Not from you," Abe grumbled.

Abe restrained himself while Dee surveyed her surroundings with apparent interest. With her every step across the dirt floor, her boots shuffled and his heart thudded in rhythm. As far as he knew, this was the first time she'd ever set foot in the barn.

He'd asked her to go riding once, and she'd turned him down without a second's hesitation. Something about a childhood accident with a pony.

"Wow, it's clean in here," Dee said. "Actually, downright immaculate." She ran her finger along the sharp tines of a pitchfork hanging from the wall. "Aren't barns supposed to smell like manure?"

Abe scoffed and rolled his eyes upward. Heaven help him. He caught the quirk at one corner of Mitch's mouth.

The barn cat ambled up to Dee and wriggled against her ankle. She looked down at the fat tabby, which stared up at her with bright green eyes as if asking, *Will you pet me?*

Abe half expected her to shoo the scraggly critter away, but instead she dipped down and patted the cat's head, earning a rumbling purr. "What's her name?" Dee asked.

"Traitor."

Dee's head shot up. She caught him with a piercing gaze. Her mouth curved into a perfect frown. He bit his lip to keep from laughing. She then turned her gaze to Mitch, who was obviously smitten. His toothy grinned stretched for miles.

Abe started to offer introductions but stopped. Why should he? It wasn't like she was his guest. Yeah, he was pickling in his own juices, but he didn't give a damn.

It was too much to hope she'd get the hint, turn around and walk out. Instead she approached Mitch and offered a finely manicured hand. Her smile looked as fake as her nails. "Hi, I'm Dee."

Mitch managed a dumbfounded "Hello," and clumsily stuck his hand into hers. "I'm Mitch. Nice to meet you. Did you have a safe trip?"

"Most definitely," she answered with a side glance for Abe. "Thanks for asking."

Mitch pushed his hat up slightly with the tip of his thumb. "I bet this is a change from the big city."

She shrugged and wrapped her arms around her waist. "It will be a nice change--at least, I hope." Abe waited for another glance in his direction, but it didn't come. "You're not from around these parts, are you?"

Mitch chuckled. "Can't hide it. I moved here from Texas almost four years ago."

"You're a long way from home."

Abe groaned. So much for peace and quiet.

Dee turned her back to him, giving all of her attention to Mitch, who seemed more than welcoming. "Did Abe tell you I'll be staying here permanently?"

Mitch glanced at Abe across the room. Abe scowled back.

"No, I don't--"

"I didn't tell him it's permanent because that's a lie." Abe shifted on the hay. "Didn't you get that much from our earlier conversation?" Damn, he really needed a cigarette. Since that was impossible for the moment, he reached for another cold one. It'd definitely relax his mood. Screw the potential hangover.

Dee smiled coolly. "Actually, after our conversation, it became much clearer that this is home."

He squeezed the neck of the bottle until he thought it would shatter. "It's my house, my farm, my life, and I refuse to share it...especially with you," he growled. The tension grew. One lit match would have combusted the air

Mitch cleared his throat and moved to the edge of the bale. "Well, I think I'll head out for the night."

As Mitch moved toward the door, Dee offered, "It was nice meeting you, Mitch. I do hope you ignore anything and everything Abe has said about me, get to know me, and make your own decision."

"It wasn't all bad."

Abe caught Mitch's smile. His frustration built to the breaking point, impotence churning in his gut.

Dee laughed. "I find that hard to believe."

Mitch opened his mouth, but Abe shot him a look that said *shut up, or you suffer.*

"Leave me out of this. I'm heading home." Mitch threw up his hands. He slid off his hat and held it against his chest as he bid Dee goodbye.

Alone with Abe, Dee said, "He seems like a very nice man."

Abe picked at the label on his beer. "I used to think so."

Mitch had fancied up to Dee as if she was the next best thing to sliced bread. Mitch was a man. Abe guessed any red-blooded man would find her appealing. He slid a subtle glance over her.

Although the changes were faint, he could the differences in her. Five years ago she'd been young, unmarked and green when it came to life, especially on a farm. She'd tried fitting in by helping with the chores, and she'd done a lot of the work inside the house. She'd even given the place a homier feel, with modern decorations and feminine touches. He'd never admitted it, but he'd liked her personal touch in the old house.

Seeing her now with her fancy manicure, long hair and perfect make-up, he doubted she'd be any help. Her attempt at knocking off casual with the new jeans, simple red tee and boots bombed.

"Was Mitch supposed to be mean and cold to me too?"

"I don't know what you're talking about." Abe averted his eyes.

"Well." She reached down beside him, grabbed a bottle, opened it and took a long drink. "You've been a total ass, and Mrs. Graves has been eyeing me like I'm the devil's child. Is this your plan to chase me off?"

"I see I've made myself clear." He glowered at her, though in truth he was more upset that she'd taken his last beer. He emptied his own bottle. "I can't speak for Mrs. Graves. I will say she has an uncanny ability to see right through people."

"If you say so." She plopped down on Mitch's vacated bale of hay and gave Abe a steady, determined stare. "You have only two horses in here? Do you ride them?" She peered into the stalls.

"No. One bites and the other kicks."

"Are you serious?"

"And at feeding time, we stand back and throw the food into the stall. Otherwise, we might get too close and lose an arm."

Her skin paled. "I know you get a kick out of tormenting me, but I'm not leaving, Abe," she said with a defiant tilt to her chin.

"You will," he replied, with more confidence than he really felt.

"No, I won't, not unless I decide to leave on my own terms. I won't let you decide my future for me. At least, not this time."

He tossed the empty bottle into the trashcan. The sound of breaking glass penetrated the air.

He glared at her. "Are you implying that I've done something to hurt you?" He didn't want to have this conversation with her. Any conversation with her. If not for the four beers in him, he'd walk out. That was more than his limit in two months, and he was feeling just a little...loose.

She studied her beer bottle and skimmed the pad of her finger around the top. "Of course not."

Dee didn't look at him. He couldn't look at her, either. He'd lived with the weight of shame, embarrassment and pain for years. He'd done a good job molding those emotions into something more useful, more productive: anger. The latter was far better than sorrow. Abe had convinced himself of her faults long ago. He wouldn't allow her to unravel him again.

"You're not welcome here, Dee."

She set her bottle on the floor. It fell onto its side. Beer spilled out in a foamy puddle; both ignored it.

Tension enveloped him. What would she say?

"Let's get past that, Abe. The reality is, Jacob wanted me here. I don't know why he did, but I trusted him."

He smirked. "You don't belong here. Did you change your clothes to prove a point to yourself, or just to impress me?"

One thin brow curved in challenge. "It'd make you happy to think I was trying to impress you."

"No." He wrinkled his nose. "No, it wouldn't." He dropped his feet to the floor with a *thud*.

"Oh, forgive me." Her tone teetered on mockery. "You're into engaged women, right? I'm only a single girl now."

Her bitter words hit home, striking as hard as a blow to the gut. He rose so quickly she stumbled back. He stalked toward her. Agitated, the horses kicked at the doors of their stalls as if they shared his tension.

Her lips trembled. "Did I touch a sensitive chord?"

Chord? Hell, she'd unleashed a flood. He caught her wrist in a solid grip. He didn't want to hurt her, but he dragged her close and bent low to her ear. "You wanna stay?" His voice was dangerously low. "Stay. But don't cross my path, or I'll throw your ass off my farm quicker than you can throw Jacob's name in my face again. Ownership rights or no ownership rights, that's my word. Got it?"

She tilted her head back and looked up at him. Her face was devoid of emotion, but the damp mist in her eyes made her a liar. "Got it," she whispered.

He dropped her wrist and pivoted on his heel, heading for the exit.

Her shaky voice stopped him. "I know you, Abe, probably better than Jacob did. If I didn't already realize you're a kind man, I'd run as far away from you as I could. You're angry and you're feeling guilty. I know, because I feel the same. I've dealt with those same emotions since Jacob died. You may hate me and I don't know if I still...if I like you much either, but we share one thing. We both lost someone we loved."

He kept his back to her, but as the last word left her lips he nearly fled outside. Sucking in fresh air, he shoved his hands into his pockets. Damn it. Damn *her*.

She'd leave...eventually.

Chapter 3

Smooth, warm lips moved across the sensitive skin of Dee's bare neck and shoulders. She threaded her fingers through Abe's thick, long hair. Her nails skimmed his scalp. She arched her back. Her erect nipples pressed against his chest. The crisp hair tickled her breasts.

The sensation brought her to new heights. She wanted this feeling to go on forever. She needed him with a penetrating, undeniable desire. Consumed by it, she bucked her hips.

He pulled back and stared down at her. His mocha eyes reflected what she yearned for. Dee whispered his name, "Abe..."

And then he was gone as cold air swept across her bare skin.

Lifting up on her elbows, Dee blinked gritty eyes and stared into the pitch-black bedroom. Her cheeks burned, and her cotton gown clung to damp skin. Her tangled hair stuck to her cheeks. She pushed the tresses aside. Only a dream, but her body tingled, rousing cravings that left an aching wetness between her legs.

As her eyes adjusted, she scanned the dark room. She was alone. Good...maybe.

She sighed and buried her face into her clammy palms. Her breaths raced; she tried to pace them. The lingering intimacy and sensuality left a distressing quiver in her gut. The worst part? That had been the best sex she'd had in years.

The mattress welcomed her body as she buried her head in the soft pillow. Memories flooded her sleepy mind. She forced herself to think about Jacob, but as always her mind thrust Abe into her thoughts with guilty pleasure.

She'd cared for Jacob, but their relationship had been a whirlwind from the moment they'd met. Their love had never blossomed and hadn't gotten any further then two people longing for happiness.

Dee rolled over and sniffed back tears. The darkness paled as a silver glow of moonlight flowed through the window. The light feathered across the wall. She watched the designs that shifted against the wallpaper. Silence engulfed her in an invisible cloak. Except for the occasional crack and creak of the old house, the stillness settled. In the city, the quiet was laced with horns blaring, police sirens and music. Someone always had music playing.

Her thoughts went to Abe, to his bedroom down the hall. She listened for sounds that he was still awake. She was deeply aware that he was close, yet so far. Was he lying in bed, plotting to get rid of her? She hoped he realized she planned to stay. She wanted to make her home here. Maybe even start a business. She wanted to feel whole again, and this was a start. She had nowhere else to go, no family.

She drifted to sleep with Abe on her mind.

The sun came up bright the next morning. Unfortunately, earlier than Dee wanted. It flooded her room with its warm light, as if telling her the day started early on a farm. She glanced at the clock on the nightstand. Nine o'clock. She'd guess Abe had been up for a few hours.

She stretched beneath the covers and yawned. A pretty cardinal stopped by her windowsill, tweeting in greeting. "Good morning to you too." She pushed off the blanket and climbed from bed. The wooden floor was cold on her toes.

Dee hurried to the adjoining bathroom and glared at her reflection in the mirror. She'd tossed and turned most of the night. Her frizzy hair resembled a poodle's do, and she didn't think even a good brushing could tame the mane.

Her boots clunked against the rungs and echoed off the white walls as she headed downstairs. Her stomach rumbled. She hadn't eaten much yesterday, and her greasy burger had long vacated her system. She meandered into the kitchen, expecting to find Mrs. Graves, but she was nowhere in sight. Dee rummaged through the cabinet and settled on a blueberry muffin and a cup of strong coffee. Feeling a bit like a thief in the kitchen, Dee quickly snuck out before she was caught.

Nostalgia washed over her as she roamed the empty house, looking at the family photos lining the walls. It evoked a feeling of loss and curiosity at what might have been.

Making her way into the living room, she skimmed a fingernail over the stiff bindings of rows of shelved books. Restlessness kept her from finding one of interest. She sat down at the antique piano and pressed the keys. The notes squealed under her unskilled fingers.

Sighing, Dee glanced out the bay window, into the lovely morning. She caught movement in the vegetable garden and peered. A flash of silver hair glinted in the sun: Mrs. Graves.

Heading out the French doors onto the patio, Dee walked across the dew-covered yard to the edge of the garden. Mrs. Graves knelt elbow-deep in the lettuce.

Mrs. Graves smoothed her blue smock over her full curves and patted her silver, football-shaped bob. Dee started to say something, and thought better of it. She turned on her heel. Mrs. Graves cleared her throat, stopping her in her tracks.

Plastering on a smile, Dee looked over her shoulder, bracing herself. "I was just coming to ask if you knew where Abe is. I'm amazed at how nice the garden looks. Have you taken care of it all by yourself?"

Mrs. Graves held up a large lettuce head, gently lifting the outer leaves, examining it closely with a skilled eye. Apparently satisfied, she dropped it into her basket, expression grim.

"Ms. Crawford, I'm not Abe's keeper. He doesn't tell me where he goes." The tight set of her jaw relaxed a bit. "Gardening is a hobby I enjoy. Some of it gets canned, some frozen. I take the extra over to the farmer's market."

Dee tightened her grip on her coffee mug, soaking up the warmth from the ceramic after the bitter woman's arctic chill.

Mrs. Graves nodded at the cup. "You would have been welcome to eggs and ham, but late sleepers miss out."

Dee squirmed. Why did the old woman unsettle her so? "I'll keep that in mind." Scanning the groves, she wished an encouraging thought would pop up from the waves of purple. She used to sit for hours staring out into the tranquil scenery. "Do you at least know when Abe left?"

"He left early." Mrs. Graves stood from her crouch and tucked the full basket under her arm. As she took a handkerchief from her pocket, she studied Dee while dabbing beads of sweat off her upper lip. "If you ask me, he seemed in an awful rush to get away."

Mrs. Graves left and Dee crossed the yard, headed in the direction of the barn. The day would be a hot one, she thought. The wash of humidity warmed her skin. The smell of wildflowers mixed with fresh-cut grass filled her nostrils. She breathed in deeply and turned her head. She caught a glimpse of Mitch walking into the red barn.

As she entered, she studied the planes of his back. "Hey there."

He turned, tilting his cowboy hat in greeting. "Mornin', Ms. Crawford," he said, his slow drawl thicker than ever.

She chuckled. "Please, do me a favor and call me Dee."

"I can do that." He closed up the bucket of dry oats and shoved it under a wooden table. "Nice mornin' isn't it?" He seemed in good spirits toward her. Maybe she did have a friend here.

She needed one.

"Yes, I believe it is." She hooked her thumbs into her pockets and shifted her feet. She was like a fish out of water. "Can I help?" He hesitated. "Unless you think Abe will get mad at you for socializing with me."

He stopped and turned his full attention on her. "Abe's my boss and a damn good friend, but he doesn't tell me who I can talk to. Have you ever worked in a horse barn before?"

"No," she admitted. She'd leave out her insane fear of horses. If she wanted to earn people's respect, she needed to step up. "But I can learn. Where are the horses and what needs to be done?" She glanced at the empty stalls.

"I'm getting ready to muck out the stalls. We do this every morning, while the horses are out grazing. Abe is usually down here helping, but I haven't seen hide nor hair of him this morning."

"He left early. At least that's what Mrs. Graves told me." Dee sighed. Abe could hide now, but eventually he'd have to face her. "I didn't mean to offend you. I wasn't suggesting that he owns or controls you." She lowered her eyes to the spot where Abe had been sitting last night. "I just don't want to put you in an awkward position."

Mitch stepped over clumps of hay and took something from a top shelf. He tossed the bundle her way. She caught it against her chest with one hand and looked down at the pair of heavy gloves. A strong odor of horse manure singed her nose. She put her empty coffee cup on a nearby bench.

"You're not allergic to hay, are you?" he asked.

Shrugging, she pulled on the gloves. "I guess we'll find out."

They worked well together. After heaping piles of used hay into the wheelbarrow, vigorously scrubbing the floor, putting down new bedding and cleaning out food bins, Mitch offered a cold bottle of water. Dee gladly accepted it and drank thirstily. She hadn't been so sweaty and dirty in years, but she felt good.

"Well, you've earned my respect," Mitch said, after chugging half of his water.

"I'm glad to hear that. First impressions are important. I'd bet mine wasn't the best." One corner of his mouth lifted. Friendly, kind eyes made him appear less rugged. "It takes me at least two or three impressions before I make my decision."

She could handle that.

After a brief silence, she asked, "Are you married?"

"Uhh..." He dropped the leather strap he was busily unknotting. "No, not now. I've been divorced for three years."

"I'm sorry."

"I'm not."

"Odd how life can change."

"Everyone experiences pain. Some get over it quicker than others." He continued to work the leather with deft hands. "Don't get me wrong. I'm not glad Edie and I are divorced, but we had to be apart or we'd end up hating one another."

The word 'hating' brought her thoughts back to Abe. "How about Abe, Mitch? How has he been?" She tried to hide her concern, but failed. "Does he sit here and drink every evening?"

"No, not often." He paused and looked at her. "He's a good guy, you know. He just needs to accept that life moves on, and realize he deserves happiness like every other human being."

"He's not going to make life easy for me, is he?" She feared she already knew the answer.

"No," he said. "This place means a lot to him."

"I'm not here to steal his home from him."

"It's not me you need to convince." He tossed her a gentle smile and a quick shrug of a broad shoulder. "I sure could use your help tomorrow morning."

"Raking hay?" She didn't mind the hay, but she wasn't quite ready to groom or walk horses.

"Planting trees."

"I'm in. I'll be out after my eggs." She laughed. "By the way, how many horses does Abe have?"

"Just the mare and the stallion right now. He's got another comin' in a few days."

"He used to have more." Once, all the stalls had been full.

"Yeah, that's what I've heard."

Dee rolled off her gloves and tossed them onto the bench in the corner. "He used to ride every morning too."

"Like I said, he needs to stop punishing himself and start livin' again. But he's a stubborn man."

Later, after finishing work and bidding Mitch farewell, Dee walked from the barn toward the house. She stopped as a car pulled into the driveway and parked next to her Jeep. Her curiosity grew as a tall blonde slid from the driver's side of the candy red convertible and waved a slender hand at her.

Dee squinted and held her hand over her eyes as a shield from the afternoon sun. She didn't know the woman, but Dee politely returned the wave.

"Dee Crawford, is that really you?" The pretty woman pulled off her wide sunglasses and tottered across the grass in three-inch heels. "I hardly recognized you."

"I...I'm sorry, but I..."

"I'm Melissa Cartel. It's been years. We met once, when you and Jacob were at my house dropping off some paperwork for Abe." She patted her big hair and sighed. "He helps with my business. I don't have a lick of sense when it comes to the financial stuff."

Dee searched her memory, without luck.

"Of course, you don't remember me." Melissa waved a hand. "Last time you saw me I was thirty pounds heavier with dark hair and straight out of a divorce. I guess it's been a long time, huh?"

"It has," Dee agreed. "How did you know I was here?"

"My aunt Rita told me."

"Rita?"

"Rita Graves. She helps Abe around the place. This is her home away from home."

Dee's eyes widened. *Mrs. Graves?* It figured. Everyone knew everyone, and they were all somehow related. In her large downtown Chicago apartment, she'd barely spoken with her neighbor more than three times. "I'm sure your aunt will be happy to see you."

Melissa shook her head, sending large hoop earrings bobbing. "I'm not here to see her." She sounded almost offended. "I'm here to see Abe."

Dee opened her mouth, then shut it. Were Abe and Melissa in a relationship?

Dee gave Melissa a subtle once-over. She didn't seem like Abe's type. Although attractive and shapely, Melissa wouldn't be a woman she could see him dating. Then again, she had no clue what Abe's type was.

"Abe's not here," she finally said.

Disappointment skimmed over Melissa's face. Crimson lips turned down at the corners, and she fluttered kohl-lined blue eyes with an actress's sultry flair. "He's always here on Wednesday mornings. Did he say where he's headed?"

"I didn't see him this morning. Your aunt said he was off in a hurry." Running like a coward, Dee added silently.

Melissa glanced at her delicate silver watch and groaned. "I really expected to see him."

"I doubt he'll be gone long. You may want to wait or call his cell." At that moment she heard tires popping on gravel and the growl of a diesel engine. They both turned as Abe's truck rolled up the drive and parked.

* * * *

Abe could practically feel the women watching him as he slid out of his truck. Women's eyes somehow felt different, like they could strip a man down to his soul and cripple him. The last thing he needed was for Dee and Melissa to get chatty. He had horse feed to unload and books to balance--and unfortunately, ignoring Melissa wasn't an option. He made his way toward the ladies and attempted a smile.

He'd meant to ignore Dee, but she captured him: a disheveled delight, her hair and clothing strewn with hay.

His fingers ached and tingled. He wanted to touch her. Wanting to tease each straw from her hair and body, piece by slow piece. His eyes dipped lower, drawn where they shouldn't be. Sweat slicked her damp shirt to her breasts. Her erect nipples thrust against the thin material. His stomach clenched; he swallowed a hard gasp. The air was too cold against his heated lips. Damn. Son of a gun. Her tight t-shirt rode high on her flat stomach, baring a slim strip of pale skin. He'd have to be cold-blooded or dead not to linger on her shapely hips and slender legs, wrapped in denim like a leather glove.

What the hell was wrong with him?

Anger shot through him like a hot iron. Was that excitement making his backbone tingle?

She must have been working in the barn with Mitch. He'd hoped morning would change her mind and send her back on the road.

Luck just wasn't on his side.

He realized he was staring when he caught her staring back, her eyes narrowed, her lips pursed as if she'd read his wayward thoughts in his eyes. He tore his fingers through his hair and looked away.

Melissa snapped her gum. "Boy, don't you look like you've tangled with a bull this morning. Bad day, huh, Abe?"

He made a conscious effort to soften his glare. "I apologize, Melissa. I forgot you were coming. I had to run get some feed." He kept his eyes on Melissa, but was all too aware of Dee.

Melissa wagged a finger at him. "Were you keeping a secret, Abe?"

Inwardly, he groaned. He wasn't ready for this conversation. "Not everything has to be front page news in this town," he muttered.

Melissa giggled. "Abe, you know you can't change a light bulb without the town hearing the news." She threw Dee a knowing wink. "And this is certainly more than a light bulb. Jacob's fiancée is back in town. People will expect you to give her a proper welcome and throw her a party."

"I'm not a party-throwing kind of guy." He snarled and shuffled his feet. He should have found more excuses to stay in town.

"But she's family." Melissa's voice teetered on a whine.

"Not to seem rude, Melissa, but I don't need a party. I know you mean well, but Abe has welcomed me enough," Dee said. Abe caught Dee's sidelong glance in his peripheral vision.

Melissa's mouth formed a perfect O. "You two party poopers. Abe, sweetheart, if you won't have a party, by all means, I will. You know I love to play host."

Melissa rested her clawlike hand on his arm and squeezed. He nearly recoiled from the unspoken, unwanted intimacy in the touch, and barely controlled himself. He started to say something, but Dee beat him to the punch.

"That's very sweet, Melissa, but please don't go to the trouble for me. I'm really a quiet person."

Cursing under his breath, Abe pinched the bridge of his nose. He just wanted the conversation to be over. "I'll give a party. We wouldn't want the whole town feeling sorry for Dee because she didn't get a blasted shindig in her honor."

Dee threw her hands up. "Melissa, it was very nice meeting you again. I'm heading back down to the barn to catch Mitch." Dee's hands clenched and unclenched at her sides. "All of a sudden I have a strong desire to use my hands."

Abe resisted the urge to pull her back. What would he do? Kiss the sassiness out of her? She'd haunted his dreams last night, and dammit, he'd woken with the hard-on from hell. He couldn't help but watch the sweet sway of her tight ass as she strolled away.

How the hell had he gotten roped in?

And on top of that, he'd agreed to a freaking party.

Chapter 4

"I'll see you soon, Dee. The whole town will be glad to see you again," Melissa called after her.

Dee kept walking. The "no party kind of guy" agreed to a party just to spite her. He'd looked like a man with a noose tightening around his neck. She sought out Mitch and lost herself in work. The fence along the blueberry bushes needed painting, and she was happy to vent her anger somewhere productive. She couldn't go back to the house. Not with Abe and his "company" there.

Dee threw herself into painting. She wasn't sure how much time had passed, but the fence was half painted by the time she heard Melissa pull out of the drive. She honked and waved as she passed. Dee growled deep in her throat. A few moments later, Mitch wove through the ordered rows of bushes.

"Think it's break time, ma'am."

She shrugged and painted another wet strip of white down the weathered boards. "I could go on a bit longer." Maybe. The paint fumes were becoming overpowering in the sun.

"You may feel okay right now, but tomorrow morning you're going to hurt like hell." He smiled gently and pried the brush from her fingers. "Not to mention you're covered in hay." He reached up and plucked a golden piece from her hair.

The crunch of footsteps made both turn. Abe stalked toward them, a scowl marking his handsome face. Dee's body flooded with a mixture of anticipation and dread. As his heated gaze settled on her, she squirmed and moistened her lips.

Damn, but that man set her insides on fire.

Abe stopped and hooked his thumbs into his jean pockets. The golden sun reflected in his eyes, turning their chocolate shade a liquid, deep espresso. The menacing set of his jaw only heightened his dangerous appeal and stoked the heat between her thighs. Even scowling, he was still devilishly handsome, sexy, and his close-fitting chambray shirt and jeans fit him like an invitation to see what was underneath. Her eyes dropped to his zipper. She looked away, cheeks flaming. His worn jeans had given her a very good idea of which way the package lay. She swallowed. She was acting like she'd never seen a man before, but Chicago had been a little short on burly farmers.

"Hey, Abe, did you come to help?" Mitch tossed the brush into the can of paint.

"No," Abe practically growled.

"What's up?" Mitch's brow lifted.

"If Dee's finished occupying your valuable time, I need to speak to her."

Mitch's jaw tensed. Dee could practically feel the warring testosterone hanging heavy in the air.

Mitch stepped forward. "Abe, hold it right there. I know where this is heading, and you should know she's been a big help today."

"She has an ulterior motive," Abe said coldly.

Mitch opened his mouth, but Dee laid a hand on his forearm. Abe glared at her intently; she dropped her hand to her side. She liked Mitch, and didn't want him to step on Abe's toes. Just because Abe meant to drive her away didn't mean Mitch had to catch the backlash.

Mitch's brows furrowed, then relaxed. He sighed, scooped up the painting supplies, and walked off in silence.

Mitch disappeared beyond the barn. Dee whirled on Abe, eyes burning with anger, and tossed her head back to glare up at him. "What's wrong with you? Mitch is a good guy, and your friend. How could you be so rude to him?"

"He isn't just a friend. He's an employee here, and I expect him to behave as one."

She exhaled through tight lips and irritably swiped her hair from her sweat-dampened cheek. "You're angry with me, not him. What did I do this time? Miss a spot on the fence?" She planted her hands on her hips and braced for an argument.

"You're a distraction. He has work to do, and doesn't need you getting him so hot and bothered he loses his focus."

Dee cocked her chin. She couldn't believe her ears. He'd lost his mind. "You're really clutching for straws now." She closed the distance between them in a few quick steps. This close, she could see the fleck of gold in his left eye, and the white line of the scar above his eyebrow. Her stomach fluttered. She wrapped her arms tight around her waist and tried to pace her breathing. Darned butterflies wouldn't be still.

"Mitch is the only person on this farm who has treated me like a human being," she said. "You're just angry because you haven't convinced him to join your conspiracy and hate me too."

"The man looks at you with puppy dog eyes." He smirked. "And you seem to have convinced Melissa to join your side."

She wanted to strangle him. "I'm sure, given the chance, you'd love to convince her how terrible I am. And for your information, I don't want a party!" How could one person infuriate her so much? Dee hated arguing, and would normally give in just to end a dispute, but Abe made her want to scream at him and claw his eyes out. "Especially one given by your girlfriend."

He laughed. His eyes sparkled and danced. She clenched her hands into fists. Did he think this was even remotely funny?

"She's not my girlfriend," he said. "At least, not in the romantic sense."

"If you're sleeping with her, she's considered a girlfriend." She'd heard of "friends with benefits," but the idea didn't sit well with her. She couldn't imagine sleeping with a man without some kind of emotional involvement.

He shifted. "I'm not sleeping with her, either. We're friends. Though why is it any of your business?"

Likely story, but he was right. It wasn't her business, no matter how curious she might be. But why did she care? Idiot. The less she knew, the better. They'd never been anything but friends. He'd kept her company during Jacob's frequent absences, that's all. Plain and simple.

But inside, she knew it had never been plain or simple between them.

"Look, whatever she is to you, I'm sure you can come up with a reason to wiggle out of the party," she said.

He shook his head. "As much as I hate the idea, it's being planned as we speak." He smoothed his fingers through his hair. His features softened. "She even has the date picked out. How does Saturday sound?'

"Lousy."

"Then it's a date," he replied glibly.

"Melissa can plan a party on such short notice?"

He glanced away. "People love their parties around these parts. They can give one at a moment's notice. They're not the fancy, swanky celebrations you're used to."

"A woman who can plan a town get-together in three days is worth her weight in gold. Don't let that one get away, Abe." Jealousy crawled up Dee's spine. Her body heated with an embarrassed flush.

"I told you we're not seeing each other."

"So you say." She grinned. "But she looks at you with puppy dog eyes."

He laughed, then, a true laugh, rich with humor. She nearly sighed with pleasure. "I guess it does sound a bit corny," he said. Yet his good humor was short-lived, and his usual scowl immediately returned "But it doesn't change the fact that you distract Mitch."

"Please, do tell me what you think I'm doing to distract Mitch from his duties. It's not like we just went for a roll in the hay. When he just stared at her, she sighed. "As I thought. You're just being a troublemaker."

He jabbed a thumb into his chest. "Me, a troublemaker?" He scrubbed his jaw with the tips of his fingers. "I think we both know who fits the bill of a troublemaker. Listen to what I say and quit getting into Mitch's way."

"Or what?" She refused to sit back and let him tell her what to do. She wasn't a child. "You'll tell me to get lost? You'll bend me over your knee for a spanking? I'll still be here tomorrow--rested, energized, and ready to finish this fence. I guarantee it."

He cocked a brow. One corner of his mouth twitched. "Are you sure you want to play this game?

"Oh, I'm sure." She tossed him her most defiant look. "Very sure." She lifted her hand in a flippant farewell and stalked past him, toward the house. She could feel his gaze following her, practically burning into her with fury. Let him simmer. She had her own agenda. She planned to take a long, hot shower and grab something to eat. She was starving.

That night, her head hit the pillow and she was out like a light.

The next morning Dee rose with the sun--but not before Mrs. Graves, who was already in the kitchen, preparing breakfast. She actually acknowledged Dee's entrance with a curt nod. At least it was a step up from yesterday's annoyed frown.

"You better eat up," Mrs. Graves said. "A skinny girl like you needs some fat on her bones."

Rather than take offense, Dee accepted a heaping plate of food and dug in like a good girl. When she finished, she headed outside, ready for another day of work, but stopped when she found Abe on the porch. He sat with his boots propped on the railing, cowboy hat lowered over his eyes, a cup of coffee in his hand.

She drew closer with a deliberate, loud sigh. He pushed his hat up and raised his cup in greeting. "You're up early."

"I thought I'd get an early start with Mitch." She scanned the driveway for Mitch's blue truck.

"Mitch already came and went," Abe replied offhandedly. He reached into his front pocket and withdrew a cigarette and lighter. He placed the cigarette between his lips, but made no move to light it.

"He left? Why?" Mitch had told her he'd see her this morning. This reeked of Abe's meddling. "He told me he'd be here."

"I sent him out of town with the trailer to pick up a horse. He'll be back in a few days." Abe kept his gaze focused on something in the direction of the barn.

She narrowed her eyes on him. "Did he know he was leaving?" She felt very much alone, knowing Mitch wouldn't be here.

He nodded stiffly. "I had planned on going myself, but thought it best if I stuck around." He took a long drink.

"You enjoy making me angry, don't you?"

"Not worth the effort." He didn't even look at her.

She glared at him. Anger made stars bloom in her vision. "Is it really so bad that Mitch and I are friends?"

He looked up at her, face blank. "Yes," he answered without the slightest hint of shame.

"What are you trying to prove, Abe Delaney? That you have the power to spite me, even if you're just spiting yourself? I'm surprised you didn't go yourself, just to get away from me. Heaven knows I wouldn't have been disappointed."

His jaw clenched. His eyes turned steely. "Say what you want. Mitch is gone, so you can turn yourself around and head right back inside. Go on about your business--*your* business, not mine. Whatever people like you do. Fix your hair. Paint your nails. Leave honest work to honest folk."

Screw that. She strode over to him and, with the toe of her boot, pushed his feet off the railing. They hit the scarred porch planks with a loud *bang*. She wanted to wipe that proud smirk off his face. She bent closer, within an inch of his face. He smelled of Irish Spring and pure man. She inhaled deeply, taking him in. Warmth tingled between her legs with each inhalation. She denied it, ignored it.

He remained cool and composed. Blood throbbed in Dee's temples, until her vision sparked with fury. "You sent Mitch away to spite me, didn't you? Why?"

"I need a reason?" Abe leaned back in his chair with deliberate slowness, each motion calculated, casual, targeted to piss her off.

It was working.

"You damn well need a reason when it makes you look like a jealous fool."

"You were distracting him from his work," he rumbled. One shoulder rolled.

"I was helping." Her pulse thundered, blood rushing faster until it nearly drowned her own voice. She stalked closer to his chair, glaring down at him. Only the clench of her jaw stopped her bottom lip from trembling. "This isn't about Mitch at all. It's about you, me and stupid male ego. If you think you can control me, think again. You can't chase me away from where I belong. I've got news for you. I'm not going anywhere. This is our farm. You can't just...just do anything you please."

Abe said nothing. His gaze dragged over her, roving from her mouth and down her body with an insolence that made her want to scream. Heat crept up her throat and flowed down between her breasts, cupping them in burning hands until they swelled to fullness and peaked. That blushing heat spread into a liquid pool in her stomach as his gaze lingered on the V of flesh her shirt exposed. He took his time, flaying her with his eyes, their vivid brown depths unreadable and so very dark, brimming with a storm waiting to be unleashed. Still he said nothing, leaving her squirming in the stillness, her fury dashing against the silent stone of him. She was powerless to stop him from raking over her curves, searing her skin. A moan escaped her, drawing his eyes back to her mouth like a red flag draws a bull.

His smile crawled across his lips, a slow and knowing thing that left her needful. Desire moved through her blood, hot and slow as molasses. "Actually," he drawled, "I reckon on my farm I can do exactly as I please, sweetheart."

Rage flushed through her like fire, shooting from her pounding head down to her pulsing, tingling center. "You can go to hell is what you can do, Abe Delaney." Anger snapped through her, turning her arm into a whip, her hand into its stinging lash as she slapped him hard across his stubbled jaw.

His head jerked to the side. His hand shot up and locked around her wrist, capturing her in a grip made of coarse-hewn rock. Slowly he turned his head back, working his jaw. His eyes found hers, smoldering with slow-building anger beneath flash-fire lust, leaving her immobile. Her breath stilled as he jerked her arm. An effortless tug of strength dragged her down, tumbling her into his lap. He held her wrist firm. His other arm snared around her waist, trapping her against his body, against the heat and hardness of him. A burning firmness pressed against her bottom. His broad shoulders hulked over her, powerful and dangerous--as dangerous as his closely-held lips, and the scent of chicory coffee on his heated, skin-shivering breaths.

"Well now, darlin'," he whispered, and his voice thrummed through her, rumbling deep in his chest. "Don't think that's the smartest thing you've ever done."

* * * *

His cheek stung and his heart beat with a heavy drumming. Anger ripped through him, but he held perfectly still. He wanted to kiss that saucy attitude out of her. He cursed under his breath as a whiff of her honeysuckle perfume tickled his nostrils. He was fully aware of his erection driving into her tight bottom. He resisted the urge to adjust himself because it meant he'd have to remove her from his lap. He didn't want to admit it, but he liked the raw desire she evoked in him. That irked him. He dropped her wrist and laid his hand on her knee. "Was that supposed to hurt my feelings?" he said through a tight throat.

"Hurt your feelings?" She tossed her head back and laughed. "I don't think you have feelings. You buried them long ago. I think it's time we have that talk we've been dancing around." She kept her pale blue gaze on him. A shapely brow lifted, and Dee moistened her lips with the tip of her tongue. "Let me ask...who kissed whom the night Jacob died?"

He tensed and suppressed a growl. He couldn't get his tongue to form a single word.

"Are you more pissed because you kissed your brother's fiancée, or because you didn't get to finish what you started?"

The gloves were off.

Since the night of his brother's death, Abe had lived with the guilt-- and tried to bury it for the sake of his own sanity. And now this blue-eyed witch-woman was ripping open the old wounds, making him remember how she'd felt in his arms, how he'd tasted her lips...at almost the very moment Jacob's car had crashed into the creek. They'd gotten no further than a kiss and a hand on her thigh, but even now the pain and self-recrimination clenched his soul in an unforgiving grasp.

"If I recall, you were more than willing that night." His fingers twitched, aching to brush through her silken tresses. He remembered all too well how soft she had been in his hands. "Indeed, you were willing and wanted my touch. You made it obvious you wanted me, all night long, and to hell with everything." He ran a shaky hand through his hair. "I'm disgusted--not only with my own behavior, but at yours. You were my brother's girl."

"Exactly, Abe. We were both at fault, but I would have made love with you that night and as ruthless as it may seem, if Jacob hadn't died, I wouldn't have regretted it."

He rose quickly. She tumbled out of his lap and lost her balance. He caught her by the hand and steadied her. When she found her footing, he quickly pulled away.

"It's all just a bitter, disgusting memory to you, isn't it?" she said.

He caught a glimpse of tears before she quickly wiped them with the back of her hand. She looked at him.

"I'll finish the fence alone. I don't need anyone telling me what needs to be done. You should do something other than sit here and feel sorry for yourself, Abe."

He thrust his hand through his hair again, this time with force. "Go home, Dee. Get the hell away from my home, and from me. Go back to your mother and let her spoil you for another twenty-odd years."

He'd meant to ruffle her feathers, but beneath her fierce look he caught the hurt in her eyes. He saw the mist of tears. She lifted a hand to wipe them, then stopped. "I could use my mom right about now, but unfortunately, she died almost two years ago."

"Dee, I didn't..."

She shook her head, sending tendrils of hair cascading over her shoulders. "If you'd known, you'd have come up with some other snide remark." She shrugged and headed off the porch.

Damn.

Abe threw his cup against the railing. It shattered into small pieces, much like his inner peace. How could he have turned into this? He didn't even recognize himself. Jacob would be ashamed of him. He'd never meant to betray his brother. There had been no excuse for what had happened between himself and Dee.

During their engagement, Jacob had been away on business trips--supposedly selling insurance--more than he'd been at home. Abe had felt sorry for her. Jacob had dropped her off at the farm, in an alien environment, and left her. At first he'd only been courteous to her, coolly withdrawn, but polite enough. Yet she'd been like a breath of fresh air, sweet, funny, anxious for him to like her, he couldn't resist. Abe had found himself sharing more and more with her. Personal things. Intimate things. Dreams and desires he'd never shared with anyone.

Jacob seemed to have little reservation in leaving his soon-to-be-wife alone. Abe had known things were getting out of control. He should have backed off. He should have gone away. He could have moved back to New York and started a new life in an old scene.

In fact, he'd made plans to do just that.

He'd gone to Dee's bedroom that particular evening to tell her he planned to leave Delaney's Farm. Instead he'd found himself taking her into his arms and doing what he'd wanted to for so long.

Things would have gone further than kissing if that dreadful knock hadn't come at the door.

He raised his head and watched her. She disappeared into the shed, then emerged moments later with a bucket of paint in one hand and several brushes clutched in the other. Without a glance at the house, she headed toward the fence. As long as she was here, he wouldn't be able to control himself.

What could he do to make her leave?

Chapter 5

Dee worked until her fingers were numb and her lower back ached, but didn't stop. The brush seemed to work on its own. The repetitive stroke soothed her nerves. The sun's hot rays shone on her. She felt the beginning of a sunburn. She was thirsty, but made do with only a few sips of water. She'd only brought one bottle with her, and rationed it so she wouldn't have to go back to the house.

She'd found herself looking for Abe. He was busy coming and going from the barn. He was digging holes for the new trees. Once, she spotted him sitting on the porch.

She moved to another part of the fence. The sun beat down upon her neck. She closed her eyes and stretched her arms, hoping to ease the tension in her muscles. A cool breeze swept over her. She opened her eyes and saw a large shadow looming over her. She blinked twice. Was she imagining the silhouette?

"Dee, you haven't taken a break in a couple of hours," Abe said. "You need to stop."

She jumped, almost dropping the brush. He'd snuck upon her. So much for her internal radar, which was usually painfully aware of his every movement.

She glanced at him. Concern furrowed his brow and silenced her vicious retort. "I feel fine," she lied. She was sick to her stomach, her back ached and her fingers throbbed.

"Dee, don't be an idiot. You're going to make yourself sick."

She didn't have the energy to argue. She stood up, dropped the brush into the bucket and stretched her back. Stars blurred her vision and the contents of her stomach churned.

Abe was quick on his feet, catching her in his arms and lifting her. "I've got you," he whispered.

"I'm fine, really," she insisted, the heels of her palms shoving weakly against his shoulders. He held her against him until she finally gave in and relaxed into the security of his embrace. His warmth and masculine scent teased her senses. She nuzzled her nose into his neck.

"Really, you're not, sweetheart." His words rumbled deep in his chest. Her breasts pressed against his body, sending tingles through her taut nipples. "Too much damn pride, woman."

Thank God Abe had caught her before she'd hurt herself. She should have taken a break sooner instead of being stubborn. He was right. Too much damn pride.

She looked up at him. Wooziness faded, replaced by something far more lethal. Her limbs turned to mush and her stomach fluttered. Fire ignited deep within, sizzling her nerves.

He carried her effortlessly to the house, through the foyer and into the living room, where he laid her on the couch. The material cooled her skin and she relaxed into the cushion, looking up at him.

Abe called for Mrs. Graves. The older woman came bustling into the living room, a frown marring her pale, round face. Dee flushed. Humiliating enough to have Abe caring for her like a child, adding Mrs. Graves to the mix was unbearable

"Abe, please, I'm okay." She lifted herself up on one elbow. A wave of dizziness sent her back to the cushion.

"What happened? Is everything all right?" Mrs. Graves's eyes grew wide.

"She's worked hours in the heat. Would you mind getting her a glass of water?"

"Certainly." Mrs. Graves hurried off with a brisk nod and, moments later, returned with a glass of water. She handed it to Dee.

"Thanks." She drank thirstily.

"You're welcome." There was a hint of concern in Mrs. Graves's eyes, and in the tight clasp of her hands against her bosom.

Abe rested his palm against Dee's forehead. She watched him curiously. This was a new side to him. "You're clammy."

He rose and disappeared down the hall, the clop of his boots receding. He returned with a washcloth in one hand and an entirely unnecessary first aid kit in the other. How sick did he think she was? She lay back and let him place the cool, damp cloth across her forehead. It chilled her skin, but couldn't touch the heat boiling in her loins.

"How much have you eaten today?" he asked. "You missed lunch."

She looked up at him. His eyes were molten chocolate pools, soft and liquid. The furrow between his brows had smoothed. Her chest fluttered, and she looked away.

"I ate fine this morning," she said. "I won't starve if I skip lunch."

"I'll ask Mrs. Graves. She won't mind preparing something--"

She laid a hand on his arm. An electrical current zapped her fingers, and she pulled away. "Please, don't."

"It's what she likes to do. She enjoys taking care of people," Abe said. She shook her head. He sighed. "Well, if you don't want her to cook your meals, you're welcome to cook. She wouldn't mind the company."

"I'll get myself something to eat."

"No, you're going to stay right here and take it easy. I'll go round up something."

"Abe--"

"Stop, Dee. You'll drop dead just to spite me." The corners of his mouth twitched.

She laughed. "I wouldn't go that far."

"Are you admitting you overworked yourself just to tick me off?" he asked.

"Are you admitting you were stupid enough to send Mitch away just to annoy me?"

"I'm not answering that. Let's save that for when we both feel like arguing. I wouldn't want to win an argument because you're too weak."

She pushed herself up, intending to move away, but a sharp sting in her palm made her flinch. She looked at her hand. A large blister had developed on her palm. Dried blood crusted in the creases and life-lines, stark against her skin. "Looks like I'm becoming a farmer, after all."

Abe's eyes narrowed. He took her hand into his much larger one. "Damn. He inspected the sore. The lines between his brows reappeared. "If we don't clean these, they'll get infected."

She dragged her hands free and reached for the first aid kit at the same time he did. Their fingers met, and the tension bursting through her veins nearly made her see fireworks. She pulled back and cleared her throat. "I'll take care of them--"

He wrapped his fingers around her wrist, gently stopping her. She blinked and sighed. "Abe, you don't have to treat me like a child."

"Nonsense." His dark eyes touched her--infinitely, deeply, possessively. "If you were a child I'd be pulling you over my knee and swatting your behind."

She stiffened, holding back a smile. "Be careful, Abe, or I'll think you're flirting with me."

"Sweetheart, trust me, if I were flirting I wouldn't waste my time on threats."

He took her hand. Raw desire joined the moist warmth between her thighs. She remained silent as he cleaned the wounds with antiseptic. His hand was tender. Tears welled in her eyes. She took a deep, calming breath. So what if it had been years since a man touched her like this?

The antiseptic stung her hand, jerking her thoughts back on track. He must have seen her discomfort, because he blew on the wounds.

"I'm sorry about your mom." Understanding glimmered in his eyes, softening them. Of course. He'd lost his father. No doubt he understood.

Dee squeezed her eyes shut and forced back tears. "She died of lung cancer. She was well one month and dying the next. We barely had enough time to get business in order. You know, the loss is just as painful when you get to say goodbye." She watched through misted eyes as he peeled the paper backing from the bandage.

"I'm sorry for what I said earlier." He crumpled the excess paper. "About you going back to her and letting her take care of you."

She shrugged. "You weren't...entirely wrong. I did hide under her wing. I just didn't want to see it."

"That's life. You don't realize how much you need a person until it's too late." He began stuffing the supplies back into the box. Before Dee could respond, he stood, his scowl returning.

"I'll go get your food," he said gruffly, and practically fled the room.

Abe was silent when he returned with a bowl of thick beef and bacon soup--a man's dinner if she ever saw one. He sat with her while she ate. A part of her wanted to shoo him away. Another part wanted him to be even closer.

Over her spoon, she watched him. He sat at the end of the sofa with his head tilted back, eyes distant. Maybe she could mend a few bridges now that the steel-reinforced walls around him had thinned.

"You haven't been riding much, have you Abe?" she asked.

His jaw tightened. "I don't have much time to ride."

"Lame excuse."

His eyes met hers. Tightness clogged her throat. Expressionless, he held her eyes for some time, cold as stone. How could he melt her so thoroughly...and ignite such volatile explosives between them? She wanted to scream.

Instead, she took a deep breath and said, "You love horses, Abe. You used to ride at every opportunity, even if you had to make time. We all fall into a slump. You just have to pick yourself up and jump right back into the saddle."

His frown deepened. He looked like a gunslinger gearing up for a showdown. She stared down into her soup. Why couldn't she find the words to make things right between them? Why did it matter? Was she still in love with him?

Her feelings for Abe hadn't been a mistake. Jacob had wronged her. He had lied and deceived her.

"Are you feeling okay now?" Abe pushed himself to the edge of the couch.

Looked like Q and A time was over.

"Sure. Thanks for your help."

He rubbed his cheek, his movements stiff. "I've got work to tend to." She started to open her mouth. He shook his head. "And no, I don't need any help. Maybe you should rest here, get your strength back."

"I would, but--"

"No if, ands or buts about it. You try to get off the couch and I'll hold you down--and we both know you wouldn't want that."

The hell she wouldn't.

She watched him walk away, then buried herself back in the cushions. Damn, was she in trouble.

* * * *

After hours spent cleaning the stall, Abe wiped the sweat from his brow. Nothing like an honest day's work to relieve a little pent-up tension. Damned woman had no clue what she did to him. If she did, she'd likely be pleased.

Opening the door to the barn, he led Sally in, giving her a pat on her rump. The mare whinnied and trotted into the clean stall. He closed the gate and slid the lock home. That was when he saw Dee. She lounged against the wooden frame and watched him, her eyes curious. She had changed her clothes. He took her in with a lingering look; her white tank molded to firm breasts, and her jeans practically announced every dip and curve.

Anger reared its ugly head. What was it about her that put him in a mood? One minute he wanted to get the hell away, and the next he was so hot he could explode. Spiraling need ripped through him, leaving him weaker by the minute.

"Are you going to just stand there?" He crossed the barn, slipped off his gloves and tossed them carelessly onto the workbench.

She shrugged with a lazy grin. "Maybe."

"I assure you, the horses are safely tucked away in their stalls." He smiled when her grin disappeared.

"That's not the reason I'm here," she whispered, each word a throaty rasp.

"You still afraid of horses?"

"My heart is racing. It may be the horses." She looked across the barn at him, her eyes dilated, her lips parted.

Damn that woman. Was she baiting him, like a worm to a fish? He wasn't going to bite.

"If you're going to stay, you'll have to overcome your fear--a farm girl's requirement."

"I'm trying. A barn just isn't my favorite place to be."

She stepped further into the barn and peered into the stall, at Danger. He rubbed his head against the wood, scratching himself. She smiled. "He's beautiful."

Abe stepped up next to her, reaching through the slats to pat the stallion's neck. "I've only had him for a year."

"Have you had this one long?" She pointed at the strawberry roan, who gazed at her with watchful eyes.

"Sally? I've had her for years. She was Jacob's horse. Would you like to touch her?" He saw her hesitation. He backed up. "We won't force the issue today." He started to walk away. She grabbed his arm. He lowered his gaze to her fingers. "Did you need me?"

Her tongue flicked out and slid across her bottom lip. He bit his tongue on a string of four-letter words. "Can we be friends, Abe?"

His heart took on a heavy rhythm. He scratched his head. "I'm not sure." What kind of "friend" would she want?

"Once, we were very good friends." Her cheeks were flushed.

"Is that what we were?"

She threaded her fingers through her shimmering hair, tucking it behind her ear. Her pale gaze met his. "I thought we were."

"That was a long time ago, Dee." He damned the catch in his voice, which was husky and utterly betraying.

"Not that long, yet a lifetime ago." Her fingers tightened on his arm.

"You were engaged to my brother. Yes, he left you alone, but that's no excuse. What I did was nothing short of stupidity."

"Because we followed our hearts?" She stepped closer.

He took in her pretty eyes, her rosy cheeks and the full pout of her lips, which were kissable pink. He remembered her in his arms and ached, a deep pull that nearly destroyed him, that nearly tempted him to do it again. "Don't look at me like that."

"Like what?"

"Like you want me to forget my anger and kiss the hell out of you."

She blinked. Her lips parted. "I'm here for the taking."

The rhythm of her pulse drew his gaze to her throat. He stepped closer and buried his hand in her hair, sinking deep to cradle and stroke her scalp. Silken tresses caressed his palm, cool and smooth and sending pinpoints of excitement bursting through his body.

He growled and brought his arm around her waist, tugging her soft body against his. She rolled her hips; her flat stomach slid across his aching erection. Her eyes glistened with a need he understood too well.

"What are you doing to me?" he groaned.

"I don't know, but I don't want it to stop."

Her ragged voice, her need darkened-eyes destroyed all rational thought. He lowered his mouth to hers. She parted her lips and he buried his tongue deep in her mouth, tasting her, savoring her. Her moan made lust speed through him like a raging forest fire, beyond control.

His hand found her chest and molded to soft flesh, teasing her nipple through her shirt and bra. He rolled his palm in circles, until the taut bead turned to iron. He needed more. He needed to touch her body without barriers.

His lips remained on her mouth while his hand glided from her breast to her jeans. With a quick motion, the button popped and the zipper slid down. He slid his fingers in, past her sheer satin panties and touched her soft core.

She dripped creamy juices, dampening his hand as he swirled the pad of his thumb across the pearled flesh of her moist heat. He drew back and gazed down at her marvelous beauty. Desire glazed her eyes. His kiss had left her lips flushed, rosy crimson.

"Your heat pours from your body."

"Abe..."

He sucked in a breath as she dropped her head onto one shoulder, arching her back. Her legs parted to allow him deeper access. He slid one finger into the silken tunnel, then speared her with two digits. Her needful moans encouraged him to thrust deeper. He jerked as her fingers tugged at his belt buckle, wrenching the metal and the leather until it loosened and released. All sanity was lost as she unzipped his jeans, pushed her hand past his boxers and found him. She clasped him in her delicate hand. It excited him to watch her slender fingers coiled around his cock, pumping him. His muscles tightened in unrelenting need, warning that release was near.

"Now," he whispered against her cheek.

Dee stepped back. He pulled his hand away from her. Her eyes drew him in as she slid off her boots, yanked down her jeans and tossed them. He barely heard the whinnies of the horses over his ragged breathing.

His breath caught as her fingers hooked into the elastic band of her tiny red panties and dragged them down her slender legs. She stood before him, partially and quite shamelessly nude. Her pink folds were visible and inviting. The sight nearly made him come.

"Fuck." The word tore from his throat as he moved back and hastily pushed his jeans and boxers down to his knees. His cock stood erect, proudly saluting her. In two long strides, she came to him. He lifted her up. She wrapped her legs tightly around his waist. He clasped her firm ass securely. In one movement, he lifted her and brought her entrance to the wide head of his shaft.

"Dee?"

She fluttered her eyes open. He gazed down into pale sky irises. "Yes?"

"Tell me."

"Take me, Abe. Fill me. Love me."

He slid into her. He moaned as her tight body enveloped his length. Her dew flowed over him, and her tight muscles loosened to wrap around him like a perfect glove. Only when she was ready did he thrust further into her and fill her to the hilt.

Impaling her, he thrust so deeply that she rocked and arched her back. He suckled her nipples, licking the pert buds until she called his name over and over. Continuing his rhythm, he flicked her clit with the tip of his thumb. She tensed, clutching him with her hold. The tight grip was his undoing. His pleasure burst from him, and his seed filled her.

Chapter 6

Dee slid on her clothes, glancing across the barn to watch Abe dress.

They'd made love and now he was back to being distant. He wouldn't even glance in her direction. Her heart flipped. His mood changed quicker than the weather in Ohio. She had a strong urge to lash out at him, but bit her tongue.

He started for the door, but before he could make his escape, she laid a hand on his chest to stop him. "Back to square one, are we?" He still didn't look at her. Dee swallowed the tears that threatened to fall. "Talk about your cold bedside manner. You'd think I forced you into having sex." Her words were as cold as she felt.

He turned his gaze on her. "You know that's not the case."

"Could have fooled me."

"What do you want me say?"

She blew out a breath between tight lips. "Nothing, Abe. Don't say a damned thing. Actions speak louder than words, and I just got a serious taste of fuck 'em and leave 'em."

He laid his hands on his hips. His jaw tightened. "I need some time to get my head together. This wasn't what I had planned." He kicked dirt up with the toe of his boot. "I'm a red-blooded man with needs. You were here and I--"

Dee stalked off before he finished. She yelled over her shoulder, "You take all the time you need, Abe Delaney, but I'm no man's good-time girl. Best you keep that in mind."

Climbing into the driver's seat of her Jeep, Dee flipped on the AC and hoped the crisp air would cool the wanton flush in her cheeks. She backed up, leaving a trail of dust as she sped down the drive.

She turned onto the main road toward town. The scene in the barn replayed in her mind in a constant loop. She swallowed the tightness in her throat. Her inner thighs clenched. She squeezed her fingers on the

steering wheel, forcing her focus on the road ahead. She'd hate to have--
or cause--an accident because she couldn't keep her thoughts on the road.

Willow Creek changed at a turtle's pace, just as Abe had warned her.
Most of the shops had been there since the town's inception. Everyone
knew everyone, no one locked their doors at night, and people believed it
was a wholesome place to raise their children. They were right.

She passed the shops on the main street and noticed a couple of new
names. Stopping at a fashionable boutique, she looked through the large
variety of clothes and picked out several nice items. She tried on a pair
of cowboy boots, and was pleased at the quality for the low price. She
grabbed two pair.

As she paid at the register, Melissa swept through the door and tugged
her wide-rimmed sunglasses off. She noticed Dee and waved.

Dee smiled. "I'm glad to see you, Melissa."

"Do you have time for coffee? I'll show you a great place." She stuck
a thumb toward the door. Her red-tipped fingers glistened in the sunlight
streaming through the wide window.

"Coffee sounds great." She'd hoped she and Melissa could sit down
and talk. She swore to herself she wouldn't ask anything personal about
Abe.

Melissa led her to the diner across the street, where they claimed a
corner booth and ordered coffee. "This place ain't much to look at, but
they make the best coffee and barbecue around. Betty Harlow has the
place up for sale, but she hasn't had any luck."

Dee's stomach rumbled. "Barbecue sounds great." She glanced around
at the outdated décor and uncomfortable seating. She mentally listed the
changes a new owner could make. She pushed the thought back as she
settled deeper into the cracked red cushion. Clearing her throat, Dee said,
"Melissa, is it too late to cancel the party?"

Melissa's blue-lined eyes widened. "No party? Girl, you've got to be
kidding me!"

Dee shook her head. "No, I'm not."

"Is this Abe's idea?" She lowered her voice. "I told him I'd do all
the work." She heaved a sigh. Each time Melissa turned her head, her
dangling sapphire earrings bobbed and clinked. Her hair, piled neatly in
a high ponytail, made her look younger. Melissa had a sexy confidence
that Dee thought men liked in a woman. She spoke bluntly and dressed to
show off her assets.

"You can tell that party pooper to quit complaining," Melissa said. "I've already started inviting people. The Watsons, are coming and old John Henry changed his poker game to make it."

"Abe didn't ask me to do this, Melissa."

Melissa's long lashes fluttered. "Okay, I'll take your word for it, but I certainly will ask him when I see him this evening."

Dee's mouth fell open. She quickly snapped it shut. When she was sure she had her voice under control, she asked, "You and Abe have plans this evening?" An unfamiliar sensation spread through her stomach, making her wriggle in the vinyl seat. Jealousy, maybe?

Melissa took a long sip, swallowed, then nodded. "He's coming for dinner tonight. Didn't he tell you?" One thin brow curved upward.

"No, but we don't talk much." No, they didn't talk, but they sure could have nasty, delicious sex.

"Abe is Abe." Melissa shrugged. "He loves that farm."

Dee squinted. What had Abe told Melissa about Dee's rights to the farm? Had he implied that she'd returned just to make his life a living hell by holding her partial ownership over his head?

"I'm not here to cause problems, Melissa."

Melissa reached up and tapped one earring. Her eyes narrowed, and her mouth pursed. "Maybe I should keep my nose out of yours and Abe's business." She exhaled. "Though I hate to think you and Abe are out there on that lonely old farm living under the same roof. How uncomfortable to live with someone you hate."

"I wouldn't say that we hate each other." She caught Melissa's look of disbelief. "Did Abe say he hated me?"

"Dee, I'm not sure..."

"It's okay, Melissa. I'm a big girl and I can handle the truth." Hurt rippled through her, only to be eclipsed by a hard shot of anger.

Melissa glanced out the window. "I'm sorry, Dee. He would rather die than have you living in his home. He can't trust you, so he's had to change all his business plans so he can stay and monitor your coming and goings."

"Monitor my coming and goings? It's a house, a farm. It's not like I can pick it up and run away, can I?" Dee lowered her eyes. She'd known Abe was upset with her--not as much with her as with the situation--but to hear the harsh reality sucked every bit of warmth out of her, leaving her cold and bitter.

"If you don't want the party, Dee, I'll cancel. I don't want to make things more uncomfortable than they already are."

Melissa didn't fool her for a moment. Dee knew manipulation when she heard it, and Melissa dripped insincerity. Dee would be happy to wiggle out of the party, but what choice did she have? She hated the idea, but at least she could rise to the occasion. She knew how to throw a party. She also realized how important the right food was in encouraging people to socialize. Co-owning a prestigious catering business that catered to the rich and famous had taught her the ins and outs of a classy function that would leave people talking for days.

Determination bubbled inside her. She straightened her back and lifted her chin. "Well, under the circumstances, I believe a party is just what is needed out on Delaney's Farm. I want everyone to hear the news. I'll be staying in Willow Creek--permanently. In fact, I may just buy this place and start my own business." Dee lifted one hand and made a sweeping motion.

"Wow, some turnaround."

"You bet." Rejuvenated, Dee flattened her palms against the dented table. "I bake, Melissa. I bake well. I'm going to bake for my party."

Melissa's mouth fell. A long silence followed. She finally said, "Abe and I are meeting to go over the menu selection." She tugged her earring so hard her earlobe grew redder by the second. "You can come, too, I mean...if you want."

"Continue your meeting alone. I'll let you know later what I'll be adding." Dee stood, throwing her shoulders back. "Thank you for the coffee, Melissa. It's been a very...enlightening conversation."

Dee took her time getting back to the farm. She'd hoped some of the anger would have subsided. No such luck. If anything, her hurt transformed into white-hot rage. She'd reached her limit. Enough guilt over Jacob's death. No more pain and blame over Jacob leaving his share of the farm to her. Enough of everything. She didn't deserve the guilt.

She'd cared for Jacob deeply, even if his secrets had left her devastated. Still she'd stayed and given Jacob the chance to tell Abe the truth. She couldn't be held accountable for that. She'd tried to do the right thing and give the farm back to Abe, but he'd refused.

What more did he want from her? One would think she'd torn the Delaney brothers apart.

She stepped onto the porch, then stopped. Who else would be standing in the door but Mrs. Graves? The older woman's gray hair was piled high on her head, and she wore black slacks and a nice silk blouse. She wasn't doing any cleaning in that outfit.

"You're all dressed up. Do you have plans?" Dee asked.

"I'm off to church." She smoothed her pants and patted her hair. "Abe is in his office. He would like to see you." And then she was off.

Dee wasn't in any hurry to see Abe. She took her time unloading the packages from the Jeep, then lingered over putting the groceries away. In the bathroom she splashed her face with cold water and brushed her hair until her scalp ached. When she thought she'd wasted enough time, she made her way down the hall to Abe's office.

It seemed awkward standing outside the open door, like she was trespassing. She peered in. The décor dripped of masculinity, from the dark wood shelves to the framed fishing snapshots, even one of Abe on a horse. Musky cologne tickled her nose, the same scent that lingered on her body from their lovemaking.

Taking a step forward, she stopped. He sat at his desk with his head lowered, eyes fixed in an open book.

She cleared her throat. His head came up. He rubbed his jaw as his intense gaze warmed her. It was a look that made her remember every moan, every touch, every look they'd shared hours earlier. She refused to allow the heat in her loins to spiral into fire.

"Did you enjoy your trip into town?" A smidgen of a smile lifted one corner of his mouth.

"I'd say it was..." She searched for the right word. "Enlightening."

"Is the answer yes?" He cocked an eyebrow.

"I've always found the social aspects of a small town to be fascinating. Everyone knows everyone's business." She flipped her hair over her shoulder. "If a person has any interest in another's affairs, all they would need to do is be at the right place at the right time." She kept her eyes averted. He'd see right through her.

In her peripheral vision, she saw his brow furrow. "Some call it fascinating. Others call it a pain in the ass."

"Yet those who complain about the rumors are the ones who spread the juiciest tales." She stepped across the room to the bookshelf and busied herself by fingering through several titles. "Why do you think that is, Abe?"

"Why do I think people spread rumors? I'm the wrong person to ask."

She turned back to him. "You're the smart one. You've got the big degree and worldly knowledge, after all. You're...what?" She cocked her head. "Thirteen years older. That's just so much older. Doesn't that make you smarter than me?"

He folded his arms over his chest. His muscles bulged under his shirt. All trace of a smile vanished.

She was in trouble.

* * * *

From the second Dee stepped into his office, he'd had one wish on his mind. He wanted to strip her down to lovely nudity, bend her over his desk and drive deep into her silken luxury.

From the angry tilt to her jaw, his wish was far from reality.

"I'm educated. I'm older. I'm not a psychologist. So tell me what's on your mind, because I can't read it. Do you regret what happened in the barn?"

"Me? Regret? Not at all. The sex was refreshing and shone a new light on things. The sexual tension is out of the way, and now we can move on."

His gut clenched. He narrowed his eyes, studying her. Something had changed, but what?

"Now, what did you need to see me about?" Dee asked.

With a lingering look, he said. "I have some paperwork I need you to sign regarding the farm. Tax papers...things like that." He tossed an enveloped across the desk. "Same things I've been sending you over the years."

"Fine. If this is everything, I'll take them with me and give them a quick read-through." She took the envelope.

He smiled. "You don't trust me?"

She shrugged. "Of course, that is, as far as I can throw you."

His narrowed his eyes. "I need them by Monday."

"Fine."

"You're going to crack if you don't say what's on your mind."

A frown tugged her sexy lips south. "Do you have plans this evening?"

"No."

"That's interesting."

He shoved back in his leather chair. It hit the wall as he stood. "I'm not interested in playing this game."

"You're going to Melissa's tonight."

He sighed and glanced over at his open planner on the desk. "Damn. How is it you know more about my schedule than I do?"

"Small town. Large rumor mill."

"Apparently."

"You wouldn't want to miss it. Melissa is looking forward to it."

He studied her closely. Her lips were pursed and her cheeks were flushed. "You're jealous," he realized. He knew the signs. No, he knew Dee. He fought back a grin.

"Have you been popping funny pills?" She wrapped her arms around her waist. "Or have you just lost your mind?"

"Then why are you so concerned with my plans for tonight?"

She planted both hands on her hips and glared up at him. "Do you want me to be jealous? Would that please you?"

"Go with me." He regretted it the moment he said it. He wouldn't survive the evening.

"What an offer. Too bad I'll pass."

"You got something better to do?"

She stepped over to the row of books and chose one from the top shelf. She didn't even look at the title. "I'm going to read this book."

Abe pulled the book from her grasp and read the cover. "You're going to read up on engine repair? After you've finished I have an old Chevy in the garage that needs a tune up."

"I find engine repair very interesting and very important for an independent woman." She took the book back and tucked it underneath her arm. "I have other plans as well. I'll be baking tonight."

"Baking?"

"Baking for my party. It's going to be so much fun seeing all the old townspeople and meeting the new ones."

His mouth nearly watered with the need to kiss the tartness right out of her. "If you wanted to meet the new people in town then you should have said something. We could have driven over to John and Ruth McDonald's place and I'd have introduced you to Jasper McDonald, their five-year-old son. Then we could have driven to the Lochbaums', and you could meet Jesse. She's three. Those are the two new members of our community." He ran his gaze over her cool eyes, upturned nose, sprinkling of freckles and soft lips. His southern parts hardened against his will. "I guess you'd rather stay home and bake for two hundred people."

"That sounded suspiciously patronizing."

"Really?"

She rolled her eyes and started for the door, but stopped short. "I've been thinking, Abe. Have you considered moving back to New York, since I'm taking up permanent residence here? The place just might not be big enough."

"What?"

She smiled. "Can you hold that face long enough for me to take a picture?"

"When hell freezes over, Dee. Don't screw with me when it comes to the farm. Just because we indulged each other doesn't change a damn thing. This place was my grandparents', and they handed it down to my parents. They worked their hands to the bone making it what it is today."

"Forgive me, but I'm only attempting to defuse a volatile situation. Two people who despise each other as we do shouldn't live under one roof. Even married people divorce when they can't get along, so why would we stay here together? If you're not planning to go back to New York--and I'm definitely not leaving--we're going to have to come to some compromise or understanding."

"I'll leave over my dead body."

"So, a compromise it is." Her sigh echoed off the walls. "And that goes for the toilet seat. Think you can manage to lower it?"

She stormed out before he could get a single word out.

Abe sat at his desk and buried his face into his palm. Why would Dee think he despised her?

She changed his mood quicker than a horse with a bee on its ass. Like no one else, she fired him up. His brothers had scraped his nerves at times, but Dee was like pure salt to a deep wound. He took a deep, relaxing breath.

He wasn't sure he was cut out for the living arrangements with Dee. At forty-two, he was dead-set in his ways. Now she was demanding he correct his habits? How did a man teach himself to lower the seat when it had never been an issue before? What would she ask next?

His buddies had been right. Move a woman into your house and the first thing she did was decorate it. The second thing she did was take away a man's peace. Dee wasn't even his girlfriend. Shit.

Abe grabbed the phone and punched in a familiar number. Melissa answered. "I won't be over tonight," he said. "Something's come up."

Chapter 7

Dee bustled about the kitchen. She enjoyed baking. She liked the measuring, the stirring and the delicious aromas. Many a time she'd whipped anger or sadness out of her mood with a new recipe. Her mom had always told her that her brain was wired straight to her nose and stomach.

During her catering career, she'd been overwhelmed by demand for her baked goods. Her mother had suggested she open her own business. Dee had considered it, until the cancer diagnosis. She'd shelved the idea in favor of caring for her mother.

Dee wasn't a planner or an organizer, not like her mother. She wasn't sure if she had what it took to start her own business. The diner came to mind. Melissa said it'd been up for sale for a while. Would the owner take a lower price?

The timer beeped, pulling her attention back to baking. She retrieved the sugar cookies from the oven. Her secret recipe. She lifted the pan and inhaled the sweet vanilla aroma.

She turned and found Abe standing not two feet away. She lost her grip on the cookie sheet. It tipped; she caught it with her unprotected hand. Heat seared her palm for only a second before she dropped the pan. It hit the floor with a clatter and cookies scattered across the floor. "Shit!"

"I didn't mean to alarm you. Are you okay? Let me see."

"I'm okay." Another blister was already rising, next to the bandage covering the healing one she'd gotten from painting.

Abe grasped her hand and inspected the burn. Dee tried to resist, but he held her fingers steady. He led her to the sink and held her hand under cool running water.

"The cookies...they're all over the floor."

"Don't worry, they won't go anywhere."

He examined the redness. The pain in her hand was forgotten as tingles of need shot up her arm. His touch melted her with yearning. She tried jerking away, but he didn't budge. "I'll live, Abe."

A smile played at the corner of his mouth. "If you'll relax, I can help you."

"I can take care of myself. You're making this a habit." She tugged again. This time, he didn't resist.

"If I remember correctly, you were always getting hurt when you lived here."

"I thought you were heading to Melissa's?"

"Hate to disappoint you. I'll be staying in this evening." He went to one of the cabinets and retrieved a vial. He offered it to her. "This is miracle ointment. It takes the burn out almost instantly."

"Is that the stuff you get from Harry Peterson? Does he still use pig fat as an ingredient?" She crinkled her nose.

"He swears by it, and it seems to work."

"I'd rather keep the burn than have pig fat on my hand." She kept her eyes on the ointment and thought very hard about pig fat. Anything to bury her mounting desire. Yet not even imagining a vat full of bacon grease could make her forget the feeling of Abe inside her, or the tingling echo of the orgasm that had tilted her world off its axis.

"No, you wouldn't."

With a sigh, he opened the container and scooped some out onto his finger. Before she could protest, he wiped the clear salve onto her fingers. She caught a thick, creamy odor before Abe's earthy scent overwhelmed it.

"Before Mrs. Graves came to work for me, I went through a whole container of this salve by myself."

"Mrs. Graves has taken very good care of you."

His head snapped up. "She has been kind," he said. "She's not an evil person, Dee."

"I'm sorry." She took the container and began applying the salve to her own hand. The creamy concoction cooled her skin. "She is a great housekeeper, I can't deny that, but I also realize she doesn't want me here. For years her role has been clear. Now the lines are blurred because she believes she'll no longer be needed since I'm here."

"Maybe she just needs some time to get to know you." He leaned against the countertop and watched her.

"True, but I usually start a relationship liking someone until they give me a reason not to." She replaced the cap on the salve and put it back into the cabinet. "She's very loyal to her boss." She bent and began picking up broken pieces of cookie, placing them on the cooling pan.

He bent next to her. Her heartbeat bounced like a rubber ball.

"Contrary to what you may think, Dee I haven't spoken to Mrs. Graves about you. Ever." He paused. "Keep in mind that this is a small town. They come up with their own ideas, as narrow as they may be sometimes."

She stopped and eyed him. "How did I become the wicked woman?"

"You're getting upset."

"Forgive me, I'm an imperfect person." She reached for the last cookie. At the same time, Abe's hand fell onto hers. A bolt of electricity shot up her arm and settled in her chest, making her breathing ragged. He leaned forward. His warm breath swept across her cheek.

"Dee, do you regret that we had sex?"

She slid her fingers through her hair and hesitated. Finally, she shook her head, feeling her cheeks flush. Abe brushed a knuckle against her cheek. His warm fingers tingled her sensitive skin. "I don't regret it," she whispered.

"Good, because I don't either."

She peered up at him. He smiled--a smile that softened his angular jaw line, lifted her heart, and made him look younger. As young as he'd been years ago. He'd been her friend, then. She missed that. Her relationship with Jacob had never been as strong as her bond with Abe.

She should have revealed her secret to Abe. For too long, she'd carried it as a heavy burden.

"You're sad again."

She sighed. "I've been the poster child for sadness for quite some time." She stood, placed the pan on the sink and wiped her crumb-laden hands on the legs of her jeans. "If I remember correctly you have a sweet tooth." She picked up one of the cookies and offered it to him. She expected him to take it, but he lowered his mouth and took a bite. He took her wrist between his fingers and brought the cookie to his lips. His eyes held hers, steady and warm. He took the cookie into his mouth, skimming her finger with his tongue. A spark of electricity jolted through her veins. Who knew feeding a man could be so sexy?

"I have a new appreciation for culinary art." His smile melted her.

She couldn't think. She could only feel as burning desire washed over her. "It's just a cookie. A secret recipe." *Just a cookie?* She had become a bumbling idiot.

He let go of her wrist, breaking the spell. "You enjoy a beer now and again, don't you?" he asked, a wicked gleam in his eye.

Dee dropped her hand to her side and reminded herself to breathe before she passed out. She nodded. Beer. Right. Beer.

He went to the fridge and grabbed two bottles of beer. He popped the lid and thrust one bottle at her.

Dee took it. The cold condensation chilled her palm. "Abe, I need to tell you something."

He glanced at her over the top of his bottle. "Okay."

"It's about Jacob--"

The sound of heavy footsteps intruded. They turned to find Mitch in the doorway, a smile on his tanned face.

"Hey, you two are a sight for sore eyes." His dark gaze slid from Abe to Dee and back to Abe. His cowboy hat was cocked sideways on his head. "Did I interrupt something?"

"No!" Dee answered a little too abruptly. Abe narrowed his eyes. She swallowed and tried again. "We were cleaning up the mess I made."

Mitch scanned the laden countertops. "I haven't seen this many treats since my tenth birthday party."

"Well, I wanted to contribute to the party we're having Saturday night."

He coughed. "A party, you say?"

"Melissa felt Dee needed a 'welcome home' party," Abe rumbled.

"Oh. That explains a lot." Mitch wiggled his brows.

"Does it?" Dee asked.

"Melissa gets a thrill outta havin' parties." Mitch shook his head. "Though, I'm surprised she's having a party in your honor." He nodded at Abe. "Got anymore beer, friend?"

Abe grabbed a cold longneck and tossed it to him. Mitch caught it in one hand.

"Why are you surprised?" Dee asked. "She loves to have parties, as you said."

Mitch pulled out one of the wooden chairs at the scarred table, sat and stretched out his denim-clad legs. "As much as that gal enjoys throwin' a party, I'd think she'd draw a line at welcoming another woman under the same roof as Abe." He laughed. His eyes twinkled. "She's never gotten over ol' stud here." He cocked his chin at a very quiet and grim-looking Abe.

Dee narrowed her eyes at Abe. He looked straight ahead, refusing to meet her eyes. Coward. "Maybe she realizes that I'm no threat. After all, Abe can't stand the sight of me. I'd say I'm the last one she should be jealous of."

Anger pounded in her temples. She couldn't believe she'd fallen for his sexy charm. So, Melissa had been his girlfriend. Figured.

Mitch had no idea what he'd just done.

"I thought you wouldn't be back until tomorrow or the next day." Abe downed his bottle of beer and tossed it for a two-pointer into the trash can. The cracking of glass mirrored the fracturing of tension in the air.

"The trip went smooth." Mitch tipped his bottle, drank and swiped the back of his hand across his mouth. "They had him ready to load up when I arrived. I expected a delay, but I was mighty happy there wasn't one. I drove straight through."

"And the stallion?"

"When I left him, he was pokin' and proddin' in his new home. He took the trip like a true trooper. He's a fine specimen, that he is. You'll be pleased, Abe."

"Let's go down and check him out." Abe headed for the door, patting Mitch's shoulder as he passed.

"Okay." Mitch shrugged and favored Dee with a wink and a grin. "It was nice seein' you, Dee."

Dee glanced past Mitch's broad shoulders and glimpsed Abe's smirk. It cut through her. How dare he?

"Mitch, have you eaten dinner? You've been traveling and must be tired." Dee ignored Abe's frown.

"No, I didn't get a chance to grab a bite. I came straight here to get the horse in the stall." Mitch pushed his hat to the back of his head.

"Then by all means, stay and have dinner with me. Abe, will you be eating also?"

"If I won't be a third wheel."

"It's your house." She clenched her hands at her sides to keep from screaming.

Mitch glanced at both of them. "Maybe I should be the one askin' if I'll be intruding."

"Of course not." She really wanted him to stay. She needed some time to calm down before she could be alone with Abe.

Abe and Mitch let themselves out. Dee began preparing dinner in a whirlwind of ferocity, slamming the knife down on carrots and nearly butchering an onion. Her siege on the onion's fortifications left her out of breath. She needed to slow down before she lost a finger.

She had no right to be upset anyway. They'd had sex. That didn't make them romantically involved. But he'd lied to her; she'd asked Abe about his relationship with Melissa, and he'd denied it. Maybe it was none of her business, but he didn't have to lie so blatantly. It wasn't like him. She'd never known him to be deceitful, or even misleading. Blunt honesty was Abe's hallmark.

Dee had tried to be honest too, but Mitch had interrupted. She sighed, lingering over a handful of half-destroyed carrots. She'd never get the chance to tell Abe her secret. Jacob's secret.

Another sip of beer calmed her enough to finish dinner. A few more sips buoyed her until, by the time Abe and Mitch returned, she had finished the bottle and left her irritation swimming at its bottom.

"It smells like home cooking in here." Mitch leaned in and peeked over her shoulder. He'd washed up and changed his shirt.

"Thanks, Mitch."

"I'll open a bottle of wine," Abe said.

Dee was reaching into the fridge when Abe's presence washed over her, his scent of spice mixed with the earthy outdoors, reminding her of the barn. Her inner thighs quivered. Need built in her loins, a steady and swelling pressure.

Her mind went blank and she couldn't remember what she had been looking for in the fridge. His warm breath swept against her cheek. If she turned her face just a little, their lips would meet. Her mouth ached.

No. Not going to happen.

She tried to retreat. His leg slid between her knees, pinning her in place. His thigh brushed against her core, rousing an eruption of tiny explosions across her nerve endings. Her cleft gorged and moisture soaked her panties.

Leaning her head back onto his shoulder, she held her breath as his hand rose and encircled her neck. The pads of his fingers stroked the sensitive skin, and she was lost.

"I can't get your smell out of my mind," he whispered.

He pulled back. She'd almost forgotten they weren't alone. Thank goodness the refrigerator door blocked Mitch's view. A flush warmed her skin from the tips of her hair to her toenails.

She straightened, took a deep breath, and forced her body to calm. Grabbing two bottles of dressing from the shelf, Dee turned and bumped into the solid wall of Abe's chest. He took her elbow. She pulled away.

"Am I in your way?" he murmured.

"Yes," she answered.

"Excuse me, then." He took a side-step.

"If there was an excuse for you I'm sure I would have figured out what it is by now."

"You're funny, Dee." He leaned in, so close their noses almost touched. "You smell like cookies...sweet and delicious."

He lingered, hovering over her. His head tilted, bringing his lips close. Against her better judgment, she closed her eyes, rising up in anticipation.

His hand brushed against one breast. Her nipples surged alive, hardening, and her back arched, but the kiss didn't come. She opened her eyes just in time to watch him reach past her and retrieve a bottle of white wine.

A mischievous smile lit his eyes. Her face burned. The man was incorrigible.

He left her alone. She stood just inside the open refrigerator. The air cooled her. She breathed in deeply and exhaled, coaxing her heartbeat to slow. Why did she let Abe get under her skin?

Stepping back and slamming the door, she tugged her shirt further down her hips. She sighed. The problem with sexual frustration was the solution.

She glanced across the room at Abe, who was laughing at Mitch's joke. She smirked. Whether she liked it or not, he was the remedy to her problems.

* * * *

Abe couldn't keep his eyes off Dee. She sat at the other end of the table. She wouldn't even dart a glance his way, and it frustrated him. She deliberately kept her eyes everywhere but on him. She certainly didn't have any trouble tossing a look or a smile in Mitch's direction.

He poured himself another tall glass of wine, and was seriously thinking of downing it when a knock sounded at the door.

"Hello? Is anyone home?"

Melissa. Abe squeezed the crystal stem until it nearly shattered.

"In here," Dee answered.

Melissa appeared in the doorway. He gave her a quick, indifferent look. Her hair was pulled back into a braid and she was dolled up, as if heading to a party in her honor.

Abe had once found Melissa seductive, back when loneliness had gotten the best of him. Tonight her bright red silk top drew ample attention to pale breasts lifted by a too-tight bra. Her jean skirt barely fit her hourglass curves. He tried to appreciate her blatant appeal, but instead it repelled him.

"Oh, hell, I've interrupted dinner." Her toothy smile and bright eyes said she was anything but sorry.

"Please, join us," Dee said.

Abe bristled. The damned woman was trying to thwart him. All he wanted was to get her alone, and she was turning this into a dinner party.

"Are you sure?" Melissa was seated before the words fully left Dee's lips.

"Certainly."

Dee got up, grabbed another plate and fork, and placed them on the table in front of Melissa. Abe poured himself another glass of wine. He didn't bother hiding his frown.

"Mitch, I'm surprised to see you're still hanging out here." Melissa tapped her bottom lip. "I'm sure you have your reasons."

Mitch rolled his eyes and stuffed his mouth with pasta.

"I didn't expect to see you," Abe said after a long silence.

Melissa laughed and swept back a tendril of her hair. "Did you think I'd let you stand me up? We've got some planning to do...and it could take all night." She caught her tongue between her teeth. Her gaze skimmed Abe's shoulders and chest, touching him in a way that left his skin crawling.

Abe narrowed his eyes. "You're the socialite of Willow Creek. You don't need my two cents," he said.

"I wouldn't mind lending a hand," Dee said. "I'd guess my party planning skills are better than Abe's." She spared him a brief glance.

Melissa flashed Dee a bright, false smile. "That would be splendid. Just us girls."

"And enough cookies and cupcakes to feed a third-world country," Abe muttered around his salad.

Melissa glanced at the laden counter. "Wow, you've been busy."

"Baking is therapeutic," Dee said. "Helps keep me from throttling certain people."

Abe smirked, but Melissa only held Dee's eyes. Silence grew between them, strained, until Mitch laughed. The tension shattered.

Melissa smiled. "Tell us, Dee, is there a lucky man waiting for you in Chicago?"

Dee almost choked on her wine. "Lucky man?"

"Yes. A jilted lover or boyfriend who'll come after you if you don't come home?"

Abe squirmed in his seat. Dee lifted her chin, the tilt of her jaw stubborn. Her irises reflected the light like a cat's, flat and cold.

"No, I don't have a jilted ex or a boyfriend." Dee smiled tightly. All Abe saw was a snake's warning rattle.

"How could that be possible?" Melissa persisted. "In all of Chicago, with all those single men, you couldn't find one worth tapping?"

"It is a big city and all of the available men are in hiding." Dee laughed tensely, but it was still a laugh. A for effort, Abe thought.

"You must be kidding. I think you just don't want to tell us all about those men you've left behind," Melissa needled.

"You're right." Dee dropped her fork to her plate with a jarring rattle. Her smile turned tight. "I'm being mysterious on purpose. I just didn't want to admit I've been having hot, tawdry sex with every eligible man I can get my hands on. It's a perk of single life in the city, you know. You can always find an easy man." She tossed the rest of her wine down and shoved her chair back roughly. "Now if you'll excuse me--" She stood. "I'm going to get some fresh air."

Melissa touched Dee's arm as she passed. "I hope I didn't upset you. I know it must be a sensitive subject."

"I'm not angry in the slightest." Dee smiled. "I only hope I didn't offend you with the naughty truth."

She swept Abe with a long, heated look. His breath caught as anger surged inside him. He'd thought she was untouched. Thought she was *his*. She'd been tight, eager and needful. His fists tightened. He clung to his anger, let it burn in his veins. Yes. Anger.

He wasn't jealous at all.

Chapter 8

Dee sat on the porch, relaxing in one of the rockers. Her breath stilled when she heard the screen door open and close. Was it Abe?

She turned just enough to catch a glimpse. Mitch.

"Care for some company?"

"Sure. Pull up a rocker and join me. Unless you plan on grilling me on my love life."

He held up his hands in a sign of defeat. "I promise I won't. Ain't none of my business." He scratched his head. "Sounds like Chicago is a city for lovers."

"Do you think Melissa thought I was serious?"

"Probably."

"Damn. I shouldn't have said that."

"Really?" His eyes twinkled in the moonlight.

"No." She laughed.

"The look on her face reminded me of a poor 'possum getting caught in a trap. You sure did shut her up."

Mitch settled into a rocker. Neither spoke. Dee listened to the night. The sounds soothed her. The sky glowed violet, sprinkled with glittering stars. The moon's plump shape mesmerized her. She hadn't seen the sky so beautiful in years. When she'd been engaged to Jacob, she'd sat on the porch for hours and watch the sun set behind the hills. The family always called it the Delaney Sunset. Nowhere in the world did the sunset glow as enchantingly as it did in this lovely place.

Staring up into the endless darkness, Dee wondered how many others were sitting under the sky looking for answers.

"Mitch, can I ask a personal question?" she murmured.

"Shoot."

"Why haven't you remarried?" Dee thought he was decent-looking, handsome in a roguish way, kind and hardworking. Qualities most women sought in a man. "Don't you want to be?"

"Are you proposing?" he asked. "If you are, the answer is yes."

She laughed. "Are you flirting with me, Mitch?" He didn't answer. She continued, "Well, at least I didn't get shot down."

"Do you think I'd be so empty headed as to turn down a marriage proposal from a beautiful woman who isn't afraid to get dirty?"

"Are you teasing me?"

"What if I were serious?" he said, words low.

"I think you're avoiding my question." She wagged a finger at him. "Don't make me pull a Melissa on you."

His wrinkling nose spoke volumes. "To answer your question, I'm still reeling from the first marriage." He stared out across the field. "We were separated for a long five years before we finally called it quits." Mitch chuckled briefly. "I normally don't talk about it,'cept with Abe. We've both shed a tear or two into our beers."

"Well, I'm glad you and Abe can share with each other. Sometimes you need someone who'll listen." She stood. "I'm going to take a stroll, Mitch. See you tomorrow?"

"You bet."

She walked the worn path from the house to the pond. The full moon lit her way. The evening was beautiful, and the lover's moon beckoned her to bask in its glory. A warm breeze shifted across her skin and tousled her hair around her cheeks.

She came to the water's edge and walked out onto the dock. Her flip-flops clicked against the wood and entwined with the chirping of crickets. There was something familiar and comforting about the silence and the water.

On impulse, Dee pulled off her shirt and shimmied out of her shorts, stripping down to bra and panties. Sitting, she lowered her feet into the water. She'd expected it to be cool, but found it pleasantly lukewarm.

She pushed herself away from the dock's edge and submerged slowly, letting herself adapt to the slight chill. The feeling was heavenly. She made her way to the deepest part and dunked. Coming up, she smoothed her wet hair away from her face.

Lying back in the water, she floated along the pond's surface, looking up at the sky. She hadn't been skinny-dipping since she was a child. Back then her biggest worry had been impressing cute boys and keeping out of trouble.

Or at least, not getting caught.

She'd only had her mother, then. Now she only had herself.

And maybe Abe. If they could move beyond the past...

No. That was just a daydream. One hot, passionate tryst couldn't erase what stood between them.

Nothing could.

* * * *

Abe stood in the shadows and watched Dee.

He should walk away, but he couldn't. Gentle splashes filled the silence. She swam like an innocent. He felt like a pervert. Why had he come? After an hour of Melissa's droning theories on love and how much she wanted it, arguing with Dee was preferable. He'd excused himself and told Melissa he was going for a walk.

He'd come down to the pond and found Dee's discarded clothes. It triggered a jerk in his semi-hard cock, and a rush of adrenaline. He needed her like he needed his next breath.

Abe watched Dee's body, illuminated by the purple haze of the moon. Her lithe limbs moved through the water effortlessly. He had a sudden urge to join her, but restrained himself.

In his mind's eye he saw her swimming with Jacob, then making love under the stars. Nauseating pain struck him. He had no right to be jealous. No more than he had a right to dream of making love to her, as he had almost every night since they'd met. So many nights he'd lain awake, trying to think of anything else. He'd fallen in love with her and it shamed him deeply.

It had been too easy to forget that Dee was Jacob's woman. The chemistry he had shared with Dee had blinded him from the truth. Jacob was never home. Abe had suspected his brother was seeing another woman. He'd hoped it wasn't true, but what man would leave his beautiful-- and damned irresistible--fiancée for days on end? If Dee were his, he was certain that he'd have a hard time leaving the house, let alone bed.

The sound of rippling water drew him back. Dee pulled herself from the pond. Abe told himself to either reveal himself or walk away, but couldn't move. He stood there, still as a statue, mortified that his manhood grew iron hard against his zipper, aching for release. He could not tear his eyes away from her. Beads of water slickened her skin, gleaming droplets shone like diamonds all over her body and glass beads of moisture clung to her long eyelashes. The wetness trickled between her breasts, slid over her stomach and disappeared between her legs where he wanted to lick.

Although red lights of warning shot through his brain, he moved toward the dock.

Dee's head snapped up and she turned toward him. She brought her arms up to cover her nudity, but as he drew closer, she dropped her arms to her sides.

"Enjoying yourself?" Her voice was smooth and rippled over him like warm honey. With an accusing glare, she planted her fists on her hips.

He couldn't help smiling. "Nice outfit." His eyes fell over her bra and matching thong.

"I dressed just for you," she responded.

"I'm flattered. Red is my favorite color."

"I'm surprised to see you alone." She darted a glance past his shoulder. "Your lover isn't hiding somewhere in the bushes, is she?"

"No, but I bet yours is." He stepped closer.

"My lover?" Her lower lip quivered.

"Don't play stupid." His hungry eyes devoured her lace-covered breasts. His mouth watered at the thought of tasting her.

"Mitch and I are only friends," she replied, rolling her eyes. "Not this again, please."

"That's how this works, huh? You can dish it out but you can't take it?"

"There's a difference here, Abe. I'm not sleeping with Mitch. You lied to me."

"How did I lie?"

"You made me believe you and Melissa aren't sleeping together."

"We aren't sleeping together." He paused a good ten seconds before adding, "Now."

She threw up her hands. "I really don't care who you're sleeping with."

"Yes, you do." He stepped toward her.

"Don't fool yourself, Abe." She threw her head back. Her eyes glistened. "We all have a past we regret, I suppose."

"I think you made your past life open to everyone at the dinner table this evening."

"Abe, I--"

"You what?" Heat burned him, a stark contrast to the cold bitterness in his gut. Any moment now he'd pop the button on his jeans. "Do you get off on this? Stringing men along, luring them, making them think you really want them?

"Sounds like you feel left out."

"Baby, don't forget, I had it once already."

She groaned and started to sweep past him. He caught her arm and pulled her against his chest.

"Let go!" she hissed.

"Are you sure you want me to?"

She hesitated. "I said it, didn't I?"

"You know you want me. You want this."

"Go to he--"

His lips crushed hers, silencing her. She pounded her fists on his chest once, twice, yet her mouth was soft and yielding, her deep moan luring him to pursue and claim, to possess until she melted in his arms. Her fists uncurled and smoothed over his shoulders.

The kiss gentled as his tongue slid past her lips. She tasted sweet, like cotton candy and red wine. He stroked her neck and slowly caressed down her lean, smooth body, pausing at the strap of her thong. He slipped a finger in past the lacy, damp material. There he found her delicate moistness. He explored her, delving into the silken wetness that betrayed her desire like a confession.

The ragged intensity of his need shook him to his core. He'd never wanted anyone as he wanted Dee. He ached to take her, to fill her, and to hell with everything else He'd have to take her multiple times to soothe his deep urge.

Her hand slipped to the waist of his jeans. The rasp of his zipper splintered the silence. She pushed her fingers through the opening and lifted his erection into her palm. His blood throbbed through his cock as she pumped him in perfect rhythm. His moan vibrated his throat.

"Abe, I need you to pleasure me. I want to feel every inch of you."

He grabbed her panties and tore them from her body. The seam ripped loudly. He gripped her shoulders, gently turned her around and bent her at the waist so her bottom spooned against his hips.

She braced her palms on her thighs to steady herself. "Yes, Abe, yes. Take me. Make me yours."

Her voice was like a wave of silk brushing across his heated skin. He slipped his thumb inside her wet passage and tested her readiness. She was dripping, and her inner muscles clenched his thumb in a viselike hold. Taking his aching cock in his hand, he guided the thick head into the entrance of her narrow passage.

He slowly slid himself inside her and then withdrew. She thrusts her hips back, her body silently pleading. One hand held her steady while he grasped her hip with the other. He pulled her back onto his erection, and circled his hips as he filled her with his girth. She cried out, calling his name. He feathered his fingers into her drying hair, tenderly gripping the locks. "Is this what you want, my sweet Dee?" His breath came in heavy rasps.

"Yes, Abe." She moved her ass to meet his hips.

Abe cupped one breast, circling his finger around the firm nipple.

"Abe," she whispered.

He withdrew from her. She twisted to face him. He lifted her thigh, opening her, and drove himself upward. Steadying her body with a hand on her shoulder, he returned to her moist folds. She wrapped her arms around his neck and held on as he glided swiftly in and out. With each pounding thrust, her moans grew deeper.

Abe tangled his fingers into her hair and brought her lips to his, swallowing her whimper. Her fingernails dug into his back as her body shuddered. She relaxed against his chest. Her clawing nails and the tight grip of the muscles at her core sent him over the edge. One final, powerful plunge, and a moan of release escaped him.

Chapter 9

Dee drifted like a lone canoe on stormy waves. The aftermath of a sensational orgasm at once thrilling and terrifying in its intimacy. Abe drew away, a hand on her shoulder steadying her and maintaining nearly possessive contact. Electric aftershocks pulsed through her, dangerous and weakening and absolutely infuriating. How did Abe so easily delve into her deepest passions, leaving her raw and vulnerable?

Fear tightened her gut. She could get hurt, and how would she recover?

"Did you get what you wanted, Abe? Does it make you feel good to make me want you? Draw me in just to cut me loose."

He reached for her, but she sidestepped and brushed past with a darting glance.

"Dee, dammit! Can we stop all the anger for just a second and talk about this?"

Dee gathered her clothes and scrambled into them. Turning back with a laugh, she slipped into her flip-flops. "You want to talk?" She tossed her hair over her shoulder and flung him her most ferocious glare. "Let's talk, Abe."

"It's not what you think, Dee." He frowned.

When she spoke, her voice trembled. "Many things aren't what they seem. There are things I wish you knew." Her bottom lip quivered. She told herself it was only the chill making her shake, not her aching heart. "You know me, Abe, probably better than anyone. How could you believe for one second that I'd slept around, especially with multiple men?"

He swiped his hand across his hair. "I know you're not like that."

How would he feel if he knew she and Jacob had never consummated their marriage? Would he believe her? So many secrets; would they destroy Abe's memory of his beloved brother? She couldn't do that, no matter how she wanted to tell Abe the truth.

Without a word, she walked away and left him on the dock.

* * * *

Saturday came quickly. Too quickly. Dee woke reluctantly. Party time. Great.

Dee dressed and braved the wilds of the Willow Creek social scene and regretted her choice of clothing the moment she stepped outside. Most of the women at the party wore shorts. Dee's light yellow sundress, hoop earrings and stylishly-piled hair screamed *city girl*. So much for fitting in.

High-pitched voices and laughter floated freely. A three-person band--guitar, banjo, vocals--set up on the makeshift stage. The keg had been tapped, and the party was in full swing. Country boys in Levis and t-shirts stood ten deep at the refreshment table, cups in hand.

Burgers and hot dogs flew off the grill as fast as Mitch could flip them. He looked right at home, with a metal spatula in one hand and his Stetson pushed back on his forehead.

Abe met up with her as soon she came outside. She was intensely aware of his warm fingers splayed on the small of her back as they slipped through the crowd. A few stopped them to say hello. More stared at Dee from a distance, until she fidgeted. Relax, she told herself. This was just like any other party. Abe's nearness was more upsetting than the stares.

Her catering career had spanned dozens of high-class parties--and hadn't prepared her in the slightest for Willow Creek. No doubt many townsfolk had a small fortune buried in their back yards, but she'd never be able to tell from their communal earthiness and simplicity.

"Well, I'll be damned. It's really her!"

Dee jumped at the booming voice at her back. She turned and came face to face with George O'Malley, a tall, brawny man with a receding hairline and puppy dog eyes. He hadn't changed a bit in five years. She laughed when he came over, wrapped her in his barrel-like arms and swung her around, sending her sandaled feet sailing.

He let her down and whistled through his teeth. "I didn't believe it could be true, but now I've seen it with my own eyes." He took her small hand and squeezed gently. "Girl, you get better lookin' each time I see you. Where you been hiding?"

"Far away, where else?" she replied. She read his colorful shirt aloud: "I'm single, how about you?" She laughed. "So, you haven't been snagged yet, huh?"

"Honey, you know I've been waiting for you." He kissed her solidly on the cheek.

"Don't let the joker fool you. He's taken," Abe said in her ear.

George squinted. "Abe, you'll ruin my reputation with the lady folk." He burst into laughter and gave Abe a friendly smack on the back. "Aren't you the dirty dog, keeping her out here to yourself?"

Abe's mouth twitched. She avoided Abe's eyes. "Is it true, George? You're taken?"

"I can answer that in two ways." He winked. "I'll say 'no' if you'll run away with me and mend my broken heart." When she shook her head, he sighed. "Then I'd better say yes, because I'm guessing Beth is my last chance at finding a gal that'll put up with me."

"Is she here?" Dee glanced around him.

He turned and scanned the crowd. "Hmm, let me see...oh, there she is."

Following his gaze, Dee asked, "The lady in red? She's very pretty."

"No." He gave his head a tilt. "In the blue."

Dee studied the woman in blue. Beth looked like a female George, with short curly hair, thick rosy cheeks and a pleasantly plump frame. As if she heard them, Beth turned. Her eyes met George's. The love between them practically shone on the air.

"You're lucky." Dee brought her hand to her chest. "I'm glad to see you finally settling down, George."

A tap came on her shoulder. She looked over her shoulder. Her heart leaped. "Lita Sharp?"

"Dee Crawford." The other woman brought her in for a hug, then drew back to look at her. "I never thought I'd see you again."

Dee cast a glance at Abe. His eyes were blank.

"I've given Abe a verbal lashing every day for the last five years for letting you leave like you did." Lita's gray eyes narrowed and her mouth thinned. She gave Abe a sour look.

"Come on, Auntie Lita, put your claws away." He kissed her cheek. Her deep, wrinkled face brightened.

"Will you run along and get your auntie a drink, my dear boy?" She patted his cheeks. He turned and cut through the throng. She called after him, "And I don't mean punch, young man--unless it's the *good* kind." His laughter rang out across the buzzing crowd.

"You look great, Lita." Dee gave Lita an appreciative look. At sixty she was thin and tight, and didn't look a day over forty.

Leaning in close to Dee's ear, Lita whispered, "Plastic surgery. Breasts, face, neck and tush."

Dee's eyes widened. "Maybe I need to get the number for your surgeon."

Rhonda Lee Carver

Lita took a bite of hot dog, swallowed, then asked, "How in the world did you talk Abe into this shindig?"

"I'm afraid I can't take credit for this. It was Melissa's doing."

Lita's eyes rounded. "That girl never ceases to amaze me."

"She is pretty amazing."

"You bet." She stepped closer again and lowered her voice. "That one has been eyeing Abe for years, trying to snare him in her web."

Dee sighed. "Seems he didn't put up much of a fight."

"Honey, if a woman swings the goods in front of a lonely man's face for too long, he's bound to take a nibble." She glanced around. "Rumor is, Abe left through the back door as quickly as he entered the front. He'd fallen into her trap, he realized he'd made a mistake. Since then she's done everything under the sun to get him back." She wiggled her thin eyebrows.

"She seems to have many good qualities," she offered.

"Don't get me wrong, dear." Lita waved a cherry red manicured hand. "I like the girl, she sure can make my hair shiny, and can't say I blame her a bit for wanting Abe. I can count the single men of Willow Creek on one hand, and if I subtract the ones that ain't worth a lick, that narrows it down to one. My nephew." She smiled and glanced toward where he'd disappeared. "He's a catch, that boy. I'd like to say he gets his good looks after my sister, God rest her soul, but he's the spitting image of his father, with those dark eyes and olive skin." She shook her head.

Dee watched Abe across the yard. He stood with a group of men, laughing. "Yes, he is."

"He's smiling. I haven't seen that smile often enough in the last few years." Lita's eyes misted. She wiped the wetness away as a group of women waved at her and called out her name. "My girls found me, Dee. They hate me since my surgery." She laughed. "You come and visit me as soon as possible, you hear?"

"I will. I promise."

Phantom fingers walked down Dee's spine--the sense of being watched. She turned around until her eyes crossed a blue, questioning stare. The man greeted her with a sharp nod and drew closer, a smile on his lips. "I bet you don't recognize me."

"I don't."

"It's Matt Lauder."

"Matt Lauder, I remember now." Somewhat, at least. She'd only met him once or twice. "You have a law office in town, right?"

"I do. Thought I should come over and give you the complimentary Mayor's 'welcome back' to Willow Creek. I know it's a little cheesy, but that's my duty." He flashed a million-dollar smile.

"You're mayor now? Congratulations."

"Well, it was between me and eighty-year-old Thomas Hawthorne. I guess it's obvious why I won." He chuckled.

"Guess so."

"No, he died during election." He saluted her with his cup. "I'll still take the congratulations, though."

"Sounds like things are going well for you. If I recall, you were married with one on the way last time I was here."

He took a long drink, swallowed, then shrugged. "Correct. Nathan is almost five, and Nadine is three."

"Is your wife here?"

"No, she and the kids are in Florida visiting her parents. They should be back in a few days." He paused, then asked, "How long do you plan on staying in Willow Creek?"

"I plan on staying forever."

"Wow, that's interesting," he murmured over the rim of his cup.

"It is?"

"I only meant that it's not often we get new blood here."

"I'm glad to be here. Everyone has been so nice and welcoming."

He swirled his punch, then sighed. "I guess I'd better let you get back to the party." He lifted his cup in farewell. "Once again, welcome back."

Dee watched him walk away. Something about the Mayor felt...off. Something she couldn't put her finger on beneath his polite pleasantry. Sighing, she brushed it away. Probably just nerves.

The evening was a blur as Dee mingled. Some of the people she had met years ago, some only once or twice. Others tonight, for the first time. Although Abe was doing his own thing, she subtly kept her eyes on him. He kept to himself, letting others approach. The set of his wide shoulders and easy, relaxed posture exuded confidence. She soaked him in as he settled into a lawn chair, his legs stretched out before him.

A flash of red drew Dee's attention. Her breath caught as Melissa, dressed in a sexy, showy skirt and low-cut top, sidled up to Abe and bent over to whisper something into his ear. He shook his head. Melissa recoiled, then fled like a wounded schoolgirl.

And now, Dee was his lover. He'd been open and giving during their lovemaking, but he hadn't made any effort to extend that affection outside the sexual realm. He had enveloped her with his passion only to drop her like a fish back into the icy sea.

She sucked in a deep breath and forced her attention away from Abe. He did funny things to her insides. Now was not the time to ponder those feelings.

Mitch appeared at her side, pulling her out of her dreary thoughts. He seemed different somehow.

"I doubt you're in need of company, but would you care to dance?" he asked. His clothing was similar to Abe's, a chambray shirt and tight jeans. Mitch was handsome enough, but no one wore the look like Abe.

"I would love to." She set her cola onto a nearby table and let him lead her onto the grassy, flat area where other couples were already gathered and dancing.

"I must warn you, Dee, I'm a little rusty," Mitch said.

"Then we'll match." She laced her arm through his. Past Mitch, she caught a glimpse of Abe. He watched her with a warm gaze that reached deeply into her. Dee's heart quickened. Was that jealousy in his eyes? Did he really care about her, beyond a quick screw?

Yet he'd ignored her all evening, despite her secret hope that he'd ask her to dance. Hardly even a glance. Dee looked away. She wouldn't allow him to spoil her evening.

The band broke into an upbeat tune. Mitch swung her into his arms; he was actually a fine dancer, and kept a good rhythm. Jacob was the only other person she'd known who could really dance. When Mitch's cowboy hat fell askew, he tossed it onto a nearby table, practically in a woman's lap. They laughed.

Without the hat, Mitch's broad smile was devastating. Dee couldn't help her answering grin. More than one woman shot envious glances at them as they whirled past, even women hanging on their husbands' arms.

By the time the song ended, sweat soaked Dee's sundress. Mitch escorted her to the refreshment table. Cups of punch in hand, they slipped to the sidelines to catch their breath.

"Thanks for dancing with this old guy, Dee." Mitch chugged his drink.

She eyed him. "You seem different tonight."

"Different?" He smiled.

"Happier."

They stopped just outside the barn. Inside the stall a horse neighed. "Different in a good way?" Mitch hooked his thumbs into his jean pockets.

"I think so."

He stared down as he scuffed the dirt with the toe of his boot. "I've been thinkin' a lot here lately, about the past. I'm not getting any younger and time ain't slowing down either. I decided to take a huge leap, head back to Texas and give another try at getting Edie back."

She burst into laughter. "You'll never forgive yourself unless you try."

"I can always come back if she tells me no." He tugged his collar. "Dee, you're a great lady. A man would be an idiot not to grab you up quicker than a cowboy ties a bull at the rodeo."

"It means a lot to me that you'd say that," she said.

Mitch pulled her gently into his arms. She gasped. He kissed her, soft and quick and with utterly chaste. Dee hugged him tightly.

"You've been a good friend, Mitch."

Heavy footsteps thundered warning. Her stomach sank. She jerked away from Mitch. Even before she looked, she knew it was Abe. His face was dark with fury. His eyes were cold. Before she could explain, Abe closed the distance between them and slammed his fist into Mitch's face. Mitch sprawled back onto the dirt, cupping his bruised jaw. Dee stared, lost for words. Abe clenched and unclenched his fist.

"What the hell was that for?" Mitch snarled.

"Don't play stupid." Abe said through gritted teeth. His dark hair was disheveled, and his eyes narrowed to piercing slits.

Mitch climbed to his feet, still rubbing his jaw. "Man, I've half a mind to kick the crap out of you. You better start explaining."

Abe stalked toward Mitch and pointed at him. "Don't you have any morals or ethics? I thought you were a good man."

Mitch's eyes narrowed. "Get a clue before it's too late."

"You couldn't wait to get your hands on her, could you?"

Dee thrust herself between the two very angry, very brawny men. They towered over her, but she stood straight and firm. They wouldn't hurt her, but she couldn't be so sure they wouldn't hurt each other

"Right now I can't wait to get my hands around your neck." Mitch clenched his fists.

Dee hugged her arms to herself. "Abe, you don't understand. And this testosterone war needs to end before someone gets hurt."

Abe's intense gaze fell to her. "What's not to understand? One night you're kissing me, the next you're all over Mitch? What the fuck is there to understand?"

Mitch laughed. "Just as I thought."

Abe and Dee turned to him. "I'm glad you find this funny," Dee snapped.

"Don't you see, Dee? He's jealous. It's not at all that you were engaged to his brother or that you may like me, it's the simple idea that he's a got a pea-pickin' danged crush on you." Mitch almost sounded relieved. "More if he'd have a reality check."

"No!" Dee and Abe said in unison.

Mitch snorted. "Have you two had enough verbal foreplay yet? Just stop bickering, admit what everyone else already knows, and marry each other already." He rubbed his jaw one last time and shook his head. "Abe, you better never question my friendship again, because any other ol' cowboy would have a fight on his hands. It's a good thing I can forgive you. Hell, I know how jealousy can eat at a man like acid rain."

Abe remained silent. Dee, too, had no idea what to say. Mitch winked at her. "Sweetheart, explain it to him when he's not so pissed off. He'll feel like an even bigger ass than he does now."

She glanced at Abe irritably. "My pleasure, though I'm afraid he enjoys being an ass."

Mitch swiped the dirt off his jeans. "Damn, these were my best jeans." He brushed past Abe.

Dee just looked at Abe. He was still quiet, his fists on his hips, his eyes brooding. She should lash out at him. Hell, she should claw his eyes out, but what good would it do? Just more foreplay. She looked away.

"You have guests, Abe. Do us both a favor. Leave me alone and go play host."

He raked a hand roughly through his hair and exhaled. His eyes were dark. "You're driving me crazy, Dee."

She blinked past the burning tears filling her eyes. She tried to hold them back, but they fell to her cheeks. "The feeling's mutual." She turned and followed the path back to the party, and away from Abe.

Chapter 10

Abe sat in the low-back chair in his bedroom, staring out at a blanket of stars against the blue-hazed sky. The guests had left hours ago, and once the majority of the debris was taken care of he'd taken his confused thoughts inside.

A soft knock rattled the door. He smiled. He'd had a feeling Dee would show up sooner or later. He rose and swung the door wide.

His breath stilled in his chest. She'd changed. The sexy summer dress had been replaced by an even sexier nightgown, thin and white. The lace hem skimmed her upper thighs, drawing his eyes to smooth, creamy skin that made his hands ache to touch it.

Her eyes darkened as they wandered over his bare chest. His cock roused to full attention. She boldly glanced at his stretching jeans; a smile curved her beautiful, shell-pink lips.

"Is there a reason you're here, or did you just come to stare?" he drawled.

"I came to rub your nose in the fact that you made an ass of yourself... but I like what I see." Her tongue swept across her lower lip, and she played with the strap of her dress.

He smiled. "I bet you couldn't wait." He'd think she was drunk if he didn't know she'd only had one beer. She was sober as a judge, and he liked her that way, completely and totally her funny, quirky self. Swinging the door open further, he stepped back, giving her room to enter.

"Someone has to keep you on your toes." Her laugh was tense. She stepped in and glanced around. "Why did I expect to see posters of half-naked women plastered across your wall, a flat-screen TV, a king-sized waterbed and mood lighting?"

He grinned. "You're about thirty years too late, minus the flat-screen."

She went to the bed and sat down, tucking her legs up under her bottom. Possession flared through him. She belonged there, in his bed. Hell, she was slowly working her way into every corner of his life. He couldn't find it in him to object.

"How are your knuckles?" she asked.

He shook his hand. "Sore." He hadn't hit anyone since he was a kid. He'd been an idiot.

She sighed. "Probably not as sore as your ego."

"I reacted strongly."

"Like a jerk."

"Don't push it. I know what I saw."

"You know what you think you saw."

"Dammit, Dee," he snarled. "Just say your piece. If you've just come to rake me over the coals, get out."

She chewed on the corner of her lip. "You overreacted. He didn't mean anything by the kiss. All you saw was two friends saying goodbye."

"Saying goodbye?" His heartbeat accelerated. Was she leaving?

She nodded. "Mitch told me he's planning to go back to Texas to try and patch things up with his ex-wife. He was only saying farewell."

Abe shook his head. "Why didn't he tell me?"

Shrugging, she relaxed back onto her elbow. "If I had to guess, I'd say it's because he doesn't like you as much as he does me." She winked.

"I am an ass." He rubbed his eyes.

"You are." She chuckled when he scowled at her. "But not always."

"Thanks."

"Why were you following us? Were you spying on me?"

"I may be an ass, but I'm not a stalker. I was told you left because you were upset."

"Really?" she asked. "Who told you that? Melissa?"

He sighed. "We are not talking about her for the umpteenth time. It wasn't Melissa." He leaned against the dresser and closed his eyes. "I gave Mitch quite the send-off, didn't I?"

Her fingers brushed his hand. He opened his eyes and looked at her. He hadn't even heard her get up.

"Now it's my turn to play nurse." She brought his hand up and kissed his bruised knuckles.

"It seems your honor wasn't in need of protecting, at least from Mitch." His throat constricted.

"How chivalrous of you, wanting to protect my honor, but we both know it was pure jealousy." She swayed her hips against his.

"I won't deny it. I've been jealous over you from the moment Jacob showed up with you hooked to his arm."

She fluttered her lashes. "You treated me like an ass because you were jealous? I thought boys stopped playing those games after elementary school."

"Not all of it." A smile played at the corner of her mouth. He laughed.

"Things should have been different between us." She circled one flat nipple with the pad of her finger. "You know my relationship with Jacob was over long before the accident, Abe."

"Jacob cared for you, Dee," he said, and instantly regretted it. He was done defending Jacob--tired of defending a relationship that never should have happened.

She nodded. "And I cared for him, but I was no fool." She looked up at him with longing in her eyes. "And neither were you. If we had both truly believed that my relationship was based on love we would have never..." She stopped short.

"It doesn't change the fact that I had no right to touch my brother's girl."

She reached out and brushed his cheek with the tips of her fingers. "Abe..." Her eyes darkened. "I think you need to know something."

The crash of breaking glass splintered the air, followed by a loud thud.

"What the hell!" Abe bolted from the room.

Dee followed on his heels. "It sounded like it came from my room."

He stopped halfway down the hall, turned to her and pointed to the floor. "Stay here," he said, and strode down the hall.

* * * *

Dee didn't stay. She hurried after him. When she reached her bedroom, she found Abe kneeling by the window, looking at something on the floor.

"Abe, what is it?" she whispered, peering over his shoulder.

"So much for listening, Dee."

He held a brick in one hand, in the other, a piece of white paper. Shards of glass scattered on the floor before the window.

Her heart clenched. "Someone threw that brick through the window."

Dropping the brick and paper, Abe stood, gripped her shoulders and looked at her sternly.

"I'm going outside to check things over. You stay here, Dee. I mean it."

"Okay."

"I can't do what I need to do if I'm worried about your safety."

"I promise. I'll stay put."

With one last lingering look, he left. Dee looked helplessly around the room, then down at the brick.

Things like this didn't happen in Willow Creek. The town was quiet, and full of friendly people. Who would do this?

Bending, she picked up the slip of paper with shaking fingers and unfolded it. Letters cut from magazines and newsprint spelled out:

GO HOME BITCH
NOT WELCOME HERE

Dee let the paper fall from her hand. Anger sliced through her. Coward. She wasn't about to take orders from someone who delivered anonymous messages via air mail.

Calming herself, she dressed in sweats and a t-shirt. Heading downstairs, she put the kettle on, set the note on the counter and settled to wait for Abe. He didn't return until the kettle was whistling. As Dee poured the hot water over soothing herbal tea, he swung the door open.

Gripping the mug tightly, she turned and raised a brow. "Anything?"

"Nothing." He glanced at the note, then back to her.

"We should call Sheriff Stansey."

"I agree."

She listened while he made the call. A few seconds later, he laid the phone back down and blew a long breath through tight lips. "The Sheriff will be here as soon as he can. I woke him, so it may be a while."

Dee sipped her tea and tried to bury the queasy sense of panic that had swallowed her anger. She couldn't panic. She couldn't cry. She could only stare into the murky cup of chamomile, watching a tea leaf bob across the surface. "Who would do such a thing?" she asked.

He leaned against the counter, shoved his hands into his jean pockets and sighed heavily. Concern etched deeper creases around his eyes and mouth. His shrug was slow and reflective. "I don't know. They'd have gotten their asses kicked if I'd caught them."

"Obviously someone doesn't want me here. They were probably at the party."

"The whole damn town was here."

"Is there anyone particularly known for being insane, violent or bitter? Someone who might really want me gone?" She sighed. "Besides you, of course. I guess it's a good thing you have an alibi."

He squinted. "No one has reason to want you gone."

"Someone does."

"It's probably just a couple of drunken teens looking to start something or showing off for their girlfriends. They don't have much to do around this town except get into trouble."

She shrugged. She'd let it drop, for now.

Over an hour and three more cups of tea later, Sheriff Stansey let himself in. After a cursory look upstairs, he agreed it was probably the work of young vandals.

"I'll take the note, and we'll run it for prints. It'll take a few days. I can't lie to you, Ms. Crawford." Stansey removed his uniform hat and scratched his balding head. "We'll be lucky to get clear prints, and there's not much else to trace this back to anyone. We have a brick, a note and a broken window and no leads. I checked for footprints under the window but after the party tonight, we couldn't use it as evidence. Abe said you had people all over the place. You say you didn't see anything at all?" His last words were directed at Abe.

"Whoever did it was long gone by the time I got outside," Abe answered.

"And you, ma'am? Anything?" Stansey scratched his head again. "Did you happen to look out the window in time to see anything?"

"I...I checked for footprints under the window...but I wasn't in my bedroom when it happened." She slid a guilty glance toward Abe.

The Sheriff looked from Dee to Abe. "How'd you hurt your hand, Abe?"

"Pest control, Don," Abe said gruffly.

Sheriff Stansey laughed. "I bet. Sorry I didn't make your party tonight, ma'am, but I was on duty. We have two deputies and one is out. He had a hernia operation, so he'll be out at least another week."

"That's fine, Sheriff. I'm sorry you missed out on the fun." She smiled. "We have some hamburgers and potato salad left over. Can I fix you a plate?"

He smiled ear to ear. "That's awful nice of you, ma'am, but I wouldn't want you to put yourself out for the likes of me."

"I don't mind one bit, as long as you do me one favor."

"Anything, ma'am."

"Please don't call me 'ma'am.' You can call me Dee."

"Well then thanks, Dee. I'm starving."

Dee piled a plate high with food and a side of chocolate chip cookies. While the sheriff dug in, she excused herself. "Sheriff, is it okay if I clean the glass up?"

"I don't see a problem," he said between bites. "I've taken pictures, so there shouldn't be anything more I need."

Chapter 11

Abe followed Dee with his eyes as she left the room. When he turned back to the sheriff, the other man watched him with a curious, envious expression.

Abe held back his smile. "Why are you looking at me like I'm the cat who ate the mouse?"

Don's eyes widened. "I just can't understand what it is about you that can draw women like flies. Must be the 'I don't give a shit' attitude. I need to work on mine."

Abe snorted.

The sheriff took a drink of water and said, "So, spill the beans. Who would threaten Dee?"

"No one. Everyone in town seemed to welcome her with open arms."

"Okay then." Stansey finished the last bite and pushed his plate away. He leaned back in his chair and sniffed. "This could be a one-time thing--a random act."

Abe leaned forward and clasped his hands on the table. "I'll make sure she's okay."

"You do that." Sheriff Stansey smirked. "I'm sure that won't be too disappointing for you."

Abe didn't comment.

Pushing back his chair, the sheriff lifted himself up, once again patting his stomach in a full gesture. "Well, you call me if you need anything or have any new information to give me, Abe."

"Sure thing."

After the sheriff left, Abe went upstairs. He found Dee in her bedroom, sweeping up the glass. The sheets were already gone from the bed.

"Sleep in my bed tonight," he told her.

She looked up at him. Her eyes shone, her vulnerability as bright and clear as a blinking neon sign. "What?"

He grinned. Not that he'd mind, but..."I'll sleep on the couch. We'll get the window fixed in the morning."

"That's fine."

The fear written in every line of her body chilled him. "Don't worry."

"I'm not, really. If I didn't run away under your wrath, then I certainly won't run from a stranger's cowardly attempts to scare me out of town."

* * * *

The next morning, Dee stumbled down the stairs and flopped onto a seat at the table with a groan. Mrs. Graves set a plate of buttered toast in front of her. "Thanks, Mrs. Graves." Dee looked up at her and managed a smile. "Did you have a nice time at the party?"

Mrs. Graves paused in cleaning the table. "I enjoyed seeing the townsfolk and catching up." Her blue-gray eyes looked everywhere but at Dee.

Dee bit her bottom lip, counted to ten twice and backward once, but couldn't hold her tongue. "Look, I get it. My arrival is an unwanted change, especially for you. But really, have I given you that much reason to hate me?"

Mrs. Graves sucked in a sharp breath. Her round cheeks turned purplish. "You're exaggerating."

Sighing, Dee stood and looked at Mrs. Graves eye to eye.

"Let's cut the bullshit. I can't stomach it this morning."

"Too much alcohol?" Mrs. Graves asked mildly. Dee gritted her teeth.

"No, but I'm sure Abe told you I had a little visit from a brick last night." Dee raised a brow.

Mrs. Graves sighed and laced her fingers together. "Yes. He did."

"I don't suppose you overheard anything at the party last night. Like someone discussing their plans to send me a little gift."

Mrs. Graves turned up her nose. "Of course not, Ms. Crawford. I would never condone such behavior."

"Of course you wouldn't," she said. "I'm sorry. I'm just a little tired this morning."

Dee rose and headed for the door. Mrs. Graves's voice made her pause and turn back.

"I don't hate you," the woman said, her face pale. "That is not the Godly way."

"What?"

"I don't hate you," she repeated with a deep sigh.

"I'm glad to hear that," Dee said.

Mrs. Graves straightened and met Dee's eyes. "I babysat for the Delaneys when Abe and Jacob were just boys. I was young then, but I still remember so clearly..." She trailed off with a flicker of a smile. "The boys were rambunctious, but with such good hearts." She sank down into a chair. "Their parents were wonderful, as well. When Jacob passed, it just tore my heart in two. The light left Abe's eyes, and I couldn't stand it. I wanted to help, but couldn't do much. So I cooked and cleaned. It turned into a normal routine after his mother returned to Florida."

Dee joined her at the table. "Abe was lucky to have you."

She shrugged and sighed. "I suppose I need Abe as much as he needs... needed me." She twisted the cloth as if kneading bread dough. "I don't have much family left--at least, not anyone who wants to spend time with an old biddy like me."

"Whatever happens, I'd like you to stay on. I'm sure Abe feels the same way." Dee chuckled. "Besides, without you I'd kill the garden in a week. I don't have your green thumb."

"I appreciate that, Dee." A hint of a smile twisted Mrs Graves's mouth as she got up and returned to her work.

Dee let herself out of the kitchen. Crossing the threshold to the porch felt like crossing a bridge between herself and Mrs. Graves. One problem down.

If only Abe could be so easy.

He'd forfeited his bed last night, but she'd hoped he would join her. It hadn't happened. He'd slept on the couch as if she was good enough for sex, but actual companionship was out of the question.

What did he want? One minute Dee thought he had feelings for her. The next he shut her out in the cold, leaving her chilled to the core. If she let herself want him too much, he could hurt her terribly. If all he wanted was sex, she didn't know what she'd do. Or was there even the slightest chance that he wanted her there--wanted *her*, period?

She'd sleep on the couch tonight. She couldn't stand another night alone in Abe's bed. His musky cologne clung to the flannel sheets, luring her with the maddening knowledge that his head had claimed the same pillow as hers.

She needed to stay busy and keep her thoughts away from Abe. For starters, she could worry about who'd thrown a brick through her window. Something. Anything. She needed something to do before she went stark raving mad.

The house could use a face lift. A new coat of paint and some fresh flowers would do wonders. After making a list, Dee headed for town, riding determination like a shot of speed. In the local supply store, she lingered in the paint aisle and fingered the little square paint samples. The myriad of shades--pink to black, orange to red, blue to burgundy--left her head spinning. Geesh. Some of these colors she'd never even heard of. What was gamboge?

She craned her head and tried to figure out what made gamboge any different from mustard. Or cat puke. So engrossed was she that she nearly shrieked when a voice said:

"You look like a sky blue type to me."

The voice murmured close to her ear. She twisted around and bumped into Mayor Lauder. He stood beside her, too close, his fingers skimming along the shelf of paint. Dee smoothed her hair back from her face, straightened her shoulders and told herself he didn't unnerve her. She forced a smile. "Blue, hmm?"

He leaned against her. His arm brushed hers. His breath stirred her hair. His lips skimmed the air over her cheek, raising gooseflesh. He dipped his head...and bent to reach past her.

He retrieved a paint sample in light, summery blue and drew it close. "As pretty as a cloudless sky," he said, gazing into her eyes.

She caught a whiff of stale alcohol on his breath, almost enough for a contact buzz. She read the name. "Summer breeze blue, huh?" She took a subtle step to her left, away from him, and peered at the sample skeptically. "I'm not sure blue is the color I'm feeling. Maybe a color from the yellow family."

"Or red from the hot family." His elbow brushed her.

She eyed him and said, "Not the color I'm looking for." *Please take the hint.*

"That's a shame." He invaded her space again, refusing to let her keep her distance. His shoulder touched hers.

Blocked between the paint shelf and his body, she had nowhere to go but through him. She swallowed past the constriction in her throat and cocked her chin. "You know, I think I'll go with this shade of blue." She grabbed a sample.

"It'll compliment your eyes."

She pushed past him.

"Have you had lunch?" He followed her down the aisle.

She shook her head. "No."

"We could head over to the diner and grab a burger. My treat."

She made it to the service counter and tossed him a forced smile. "That's nice of you, but I'd like to get back home and get started painting. Lots to do, you know."

"Dinner?" he persisted.

The young female clerk flipped a curious look from Dee to Matt. Dee handed her the sample. To the Mayor, she said, "Maybe you and your wife could come out to the farm for dinner one evening. I'd love to meet her. The last time I was in Willow Creek, I believe she was away most of the time."

"I can help paint if you'd like."

Irritation made her tense. "When is your wife coming home?"

He leaned against the counter, stuck a hand into his pocket and crossed his feet at the ankles He did have a certain charm, which likely turned some women to mush, but it only repulsed Dee.

"She's decided to stay and visit her family a few more days." He held her eyes and lowered his voice. "I'm getting lonely in that big house of mine. It would sure be nice to have some company."

Dee bit back a laugh. "You seem to know what you want. Good luck with that," she said.

"Maybe I'll come out to the farm one evening to visit."

"That's a good idea. I bet Abe would love to have your company."

Matt tensed. He pulled his hand from front pocket and pushed away from the counter. "Happy painting." With a smile, dark with promise, he walked away and left the store.

"He's cute, isn't he?" The girl behind the counter pried open the top to the paint can.

"I guess, if he's your type."

"He's not yours?" the girl asked.

Dee sighed. "Right now, I'm not sure what my type is."

She avoided further questions by feigning intense interest in a few carpet swatches. Once the girl had finished with her paint, Dee checked off the rest of the list and left the store with laden arms. She nearly dropped a trail of bags across the parking lot--until Sheriff Stansey caught up with her, practically stumbling across the pavement.

"Let me get that," he panted, retrieving a few bags with sweaty fingers.

"Thanks," she said, and led him toward her Jeep. "Were you at the diner?"

"Yep. Just finished lunch. Thought I'd burn off a few calories." His breathing evened out. "You get your window fixed?"

"Not yet. Tomorrow, though." At her Jeep, she loaded the bags and cans into the back seat.

"The brick was probably a one-time case, Dee." He scratched his chin. "There were no other reports of vandalism anywhere else in the county last night."

Although a brick through a window was a premeditated act, Dee knew it was a lost cause. It had been disturbing, but she would let it go. What choice did she have? "You and Abe are probably right. It was a group of teens looking for something to do."

He nodded. "Kids will be kids."

"Thanks for the help, Sheriff." She climbed into the driver's seat. "Come out to the farm for dinner soon."

"I'd like that. I don't get many home cooked meals, I'm afraid--unless you consider the greasy pork chops and potatoes they serve over at the diner. As you see, I eat there a lot." He palmed his large stomach.

She laughed and started the engine. As she pulled away, she wondered if the incident had truly been a prank. If not, the next time might be more serious.

Abe's truck wasn't in the driveway when she returned. She noticed Mrs. Graves fiddling in the garden. Rather than push her luck with the older woman by asking if she needed help, Dee went upstairs, laid out her supplies and set to work.

For the first time since she arrived at Delaney's, she had a sense of being home.

Chapter 12

Abe followed the paint fumes upstairs to Dee's bedroom. She went about her business, with no idea she was being watched.

He thoroughly enjoyed his view. Watching her intrigued him. With each roll of the brush, she pursed her lips. Her hair was pulled back into a ponytail, making her look youthful. Her face was bare of make-up. She wore baggy, worn cutoffs and a yellow tank. To him, she'd never looked sexier.

His eyes dropped to her bare feet. Her red-painted toes curled on the plastic she'd laid down. When she lifted herself on tiptoes to reach, her ass tightened. Not even the slack shorts could hide the firm muscle.

He'd had a hard-on since she'd arrived in Willow Creek, and the few times they'd given in to pleasure hadn't come close to sating the urgent need in his bones. Last night he'd left her in his bed alone. A huge part of him had wished she'd asked him to stay with her. He would have been happy holding her.

She bent to absorb more paint with the roller. A surge of excitement rippled through his body. It was more than sexual. Something deep welled inside him, a feeling he wasn't prepared to face. Yet he couldn't escape his relief. If she was painting, she was planning to stay.

Her gaze caught him. A flash of a smile lifted the corners of her mouth. "Abe, how long have you been standing there?"

He shrugged and pushed his body away from the doorframe. His emotions were a bit...vulnerable. He needed a moment to gather his senses. Taking a deep breath and exhaling slowly, he said roughly, "Maybe you should have consulted me before painting the walls powder blue."

She rolled her eyes. "Consulted you on the color of *my* walls in *my* bedroom?" She went back to painting. "I'll be sure to ask your opinion before I begin the living room."

"Yeah?" He smiled against his will.

She shot him a rebellious look over her shoulder. "I bought two cans of light green. There's a brush if you want to jump in and help."

He sighed. "Well, at least it's not this blue shit that reminds me of a tampon box."

She dropped her roller back into the paint. "If you knew anything about style you'd have painted those pea green walls in your bedroom years ago."

He couldn't argue with that. The walls hadn't been painted since he was a boy, and showed their age. "Melissa had begged me to make some changes around here." The words fell out of their own accord. One look at her face promised he was in trouble.

"Melissa will be pleased." She turned her back on him.

"Don't be pissed, Dee." Figured. He'd tried to push her away and, when he'd succeeded, wanted her close again. She left him spinning.

"Summer breeze," she said flatly.

"Huh?"

"The paint is called summer breeze, not powder blue. And though you may think it looks prissy, it looks good to me. So did you come here for a reason?"

"Don't remember now." He couldn't remember anything past the pulsating in his brain. "I've gotta go take a shower. I have a meeting in town in an hour."

"Have fun."

* * * *

Several hours later, Dee laid down the brush. Her muscles ached, and she could've fallen asleep standing. She took a long, hot shower and didn't leave the water until it was unbearably cold.

She dressed, brushed out her wet hair, and went downstairs to find the house empty. Abe was still in town, and Mrs. Graves was gone for the evening.

After fixing herself a small bite to eat, she settled down on the couch with a cup of tea and one of the books from Abe's office.

The worn cover reminded her that Abe loved to read. Few people knew he'd graduated with a master's degree in business, and owned many small businesses in town. He could take anything and mold it into prosperity.

The shrill ring of the phone made her jump. As she reached for the cordless, the book slipped from her lap and fell with a loud thud. A loose piece of paper floated across the floor and disappeared. She got to the phone just as the ringing stopped.

What had that piece of paper been? Where had it fallen?

She spotted it by the couch. Sinking to her hands and knees, she reached for it. A surge of wind blew through the open window and swept the paper underneath.

Frustrated, she stretched her back and arms and pulled it out. It was a photo. She lifted it into the lamplight and smiled. It was a picture of her, Jacob and Abe, taken a few days after she had come to the farm. She stood between the two men, who towered over her small frame.

They'd been celebrating Jacob's birthday. Dee had made him cupcakes, because he'd told her he missed the confections his mother used to make for their birthdays. In the snapshot, she held a cake proudly. Abe and Jacob both had a dab of green icing on the tips of their noses.

Dee didn't realize that she was crying until a tear fell onto the picture. She quickly wiped the wetness from the shiny surface with her shirt. She was staring at the image when the lights blinked once, twice--then everything went pitch dark.

"Damn!"

She wondered if a storm brewed. Ohio was known for its sudden torrential downpours, causing blackouts. She doubted it was the weather.

The sliver of moonlight filtering in through the curtain provided sufficient light to find her way through the room and look outside. Oddly, the security lights along the grove and barn were still on. She didn't know much about electricity and all its complicated aspects, but she guessed if the security lights were still on, it wasn't a wide-spread outage. The lights were out only in the house.

She started to turn away when the flash of a dark shadow in the yard caught her attention. She studied the area with slitted eyes, but saw nothing. Were her eyes playing tricks on her?

Just when she'd chalked it up to a vivid imagination, she saw it again. She leaned in closer. The fat tabby cat flounced up on the windowsill and let out a long meow. Dee almost jumped out of her skin. She grabbed her chest.

"You scared the hell out of me, cat." She got another pitiful meow in response. Dee laughed. She was being silly.

What should she do? She could sit in the dark and wait for Abe or take matters into her own hands, find the fuse box, flip the switch and hope that solved the problem.

Using the light on her cellphone, Dee fumbled through the kitchen to the laundry room in search of a flashlight. Opening the door, she flashed the cell into the pitch-black room. Without windows, the makeshift light did little to help her see.

Something struck her calves. She tumbled to her knees and struck her head on the corner of the washer. Her cellphone flew across the room, skittering into the dark. A dull ache throbbed on her forehead. She touched her forehead, feeling over the bump. It was small, with no wetness--no blood. She'd survive.

She sat up, shoved the laundry basket she'd tripped over with her foot and groped through the shadows until she found the metal toolbox on the floor. Rummaging inside, working by touch, she dug a flashlight from the bottom and flicked it on. Its broad beam eased her tension.

On hands and knees again, she scanned the room for her phone. Seeing the light from under the dryer, she crouched down low, pressed her cheek to the cool wood floor and attempted to reach it. No use.

Standing, she swept her clothes for spiders. She stiffened at a sound from the kitchen and listened closely Another muffled sound broke the silence. She crept to the doorway. "Abe? Hello? Is anyone there?" The thick calm greeted her. She headed for the basement, light in hand and a sharp eye out for further obstacles.

At the door she paused. Should she wait for Abe?

He could go straight to the fuse box and fix the problem much quicker than she. But how long would he be gone? She didn't like waiting in the dark. She'd rather get the lights on as soon as possible.

Dee took a step onto the top rung and shone the light around the darkness. A cold blast of musky air wafted across her face. Trepidation slithered up her spine. Better than spiders, mice, or other creepy crawlies, though in truth, the darkness frightened her more.

"Grow up, Dee."

Taking a deep breath, she exhaled slowly. She pushed through the fear and moved down each step. The concrete room was cool and dank. She shuddered.

She moved the light around the walls, looking for a metal box. The quicker she found it and flipped the circuit, the faster she could get back upstairs to a friendlier, more bug-free environment.

Boxes lined each wall, stacked as high as she was tall. Broken furniture, antiques and useless junk blocked her way. She was ready to give up when the light reflected off something shiny between two stacks of boxes.

Dee pushed past a broken rocking chair, a ratty table and a large box and slid precariously between two pieces of furniture, finally squeezing through to the fuse box.

Silken webs surrounded her, clinging to her skin and snagging in her hair. Great. To make matters worse, she wasn't even sure this would work.

She pried the box open and peered inside at the fuses. Not one was clearly marked; she flicked a few at random. Nothing happened.

"Think, Dee." Tinkering with the switches wouldn't make a difference if she had no idea it was working. Dee forced back through the narrow path and searched for the hanging chain for the ceiling light. She found it, pulled, but it didn't work. Still no lights.

She started for the stairs. Several thunderous creaks came from the floor above, followed by a loud *thud*. She held her breath and waited. Another clunk came, then a loud squeak. The basement door shut with a resounding *click*. Alarm punched through her.

"Abe?" she called.

No answer.

Her heartbeat rose to a booming rumble. She'd heard someone, without a doubt. That hadn't been the natural creak of an old house settling. She darted up the stairs and bolted to the closed door. She turned the rusty knob. Nothing. She tried again, but it wouldn't open.

The door was locked.

She pounded with one fist while still maintaining a grip on the flashlight. "I'm down here, Abe! Mrs. Graves? Who's there?"

Paranoia ate at her nerves. The darkness closed around her, squeezing her heart until her blood pressure rose, pulse pounding. Anything could be in the darkness. Things with crawling feelers, sharp fangs, grasping hands. No exit. The basement's trap was a noose tightening around her neck. Deep breaths. Abe would be home soon. This was temporary. She could do this. Stop worrying about what was in the basement. The real question was, why had the door closed in the first place? Who had locked it?

And where had they gone?

An eerie sensation washed over her. She wasn't alone. She remembered the shadow she had seen outside. Maybe it hadn't been a figment of her imagination.

She pressed an ear to the door and listened for any sound on the other side. Watching all those scary movies as a teen didn't help in situations like this.

Dee told herself to be logical. There was no one in the house. She was alone. There wasn't anyone out there, and the electricity hadn't been cut off. No one had shut and locked the door on her. She laughed, but it was weak even to her own ears.

"Okay, Dee. Relax," she whispered. She had her flashlight and, dim though it was, it gave her some security.

She'd never considered herself particularly lucky, but tonight the last of her luck must have run dry. The flashlight flickered, faded and died. Darkness plunged down.

"Oh, no." She frantically banged the light against her palm. A firm shake only confirmed it was dead. From her perch on the top step, she could see nothing, not even inches in front of her face.

Dee closed her eyes. The scents of dust and mildew wrapped around her as the darkness heightened her other senses. Cracks and pops were loud and distinct, eerie. Concrete coolness nearly caressed her skin. The wind, blowing hard outside, whistled through the one small window.

She'd have to just sit and wait it out.

With each passing minute she grew colder and more anxious. She listened intently. She hoped Abe would hurry, and wished she had her phone.

What if Abe didn't come home? She couldn't sleep in the basement all night. The idea sent shivers through her. She began to cry.

Dee pounded on the door until her hands bruised. She yelled until her voice broke into raspy whispers. No one answered. Still she cried, shouting until she grew too tired to even lift her arm for another strike.

Sinking against the door, she closed her eyes and gave up.

Chapter 13

Abe opened the front door to the house. Darkness met him, filling him with eerie apprehension.

The house seemed empty, yet he was fairly sure Dee was home. Her car was in the drive. At just after ten, he doubted she was in bed. In the foyer, he tried the table lamp. Nothing happened. The electricity was out. He glanced outside; the security lights were on. Odd. He pulled out the mini flashlight hooked to his keychain and turned it on.

Abe moved into the living room. He caught a whiff of Dee's honeysuckle scent lingering in the air. He walked around the couch. His boot caught something on the floor. He bent to pick it up, and his heart skipped a beat. The book from his office. Had she found the picture he kept hidden there?

"Dee?" No answer. He hurried upstairs, checking in her room, then his and the bathroom. There was no sign of her. His breathing grew rapid and hoarse. His pulse raced. He stopped at his bedside table and grabbed the flashlight.

Where could she be?

Abe hurried back downstairs, searching every room frantically. His concern tripled. He cursed himself for leaving her. He stopped in the middle of the kitchen and shot the light from corner to corner. Nothing. He had checked every room except the basement.

The door to the basement was locked. He started to walk away, but instinct warned him to check it anyway. He clicked the lock and opened the door. Dee fell into a heap at his feet.

"Dee?" He dropped the light as he knelt next to her.

Her eyes fluttered open. She moaned, then jerked completely awake. "Abe, where the hell have you been?"

"Are you okay? Why were you sleeping in the basement?" He helped her sit up and cuddled her in the crook of his elbow.

"I just thought I'd take a nap on the basement stairs," she rasped.

"That's not funny."

"You're damn right it's not funny." She pushed up from the floor and swiped the seat of her pants. "I've been stuck down there in that dark dungeon for who freaking knows how long. I've probably got spiders in my hair, in my shirt and maybe even down my pants."

"Why didn't you call me?"

She clenched her jaw. "Because I lost my phone under the dryer. I couldn't reach it."

"It's ok now, sweetheart. Calm down. You're shaking. Tell me what happened." He tightened his embrace, even when she glared at him. He didn't want to let her go.

"Calm down? Don't tell me to calm down, Abe! Someone locked me in the basement. I went to look at the fuse box. I heard a noise, and the next thing I know the door was closed. I couldn't get out." She pinched the bridge of her nose. "Did you check the house?" She quickly scanned the dimness, as if looking for someone hiding in the shadows. Her arms wrapped around her body.

"I searched the house when I was looking for you. I saw no one." He picked up the flashlight and shone it into the open basement door. "Are you sure you didn't shut the door behind you? It has a safety lock that automatically locks when it closes."

"I'm sure I didn't shut it."

"I believe you." He closed the thick door, checked the lock, then took her hand in his and led her toward the stairs. "Let's get you safe and sound. Then I'll have another look around."

"No." She ground her feet into the floor and refused to budge. "Let's go together." The fear in her eyes cut through him.

"Okay, we'll take a look at all the doors and windows to make sure they're secure." Later, when he was sure Dee was all right, he'd check the perimeter of the house.

"Okay."

A half hour later turned up nothing except her phone, which Abe had managed to retrieve with a broom handle. They ended their exploration upstairs in his bedroom. Abe pulled down the covers on his bed. "Climb in."

He lit candles, setting the room aglow. He switched off the flashlight, placed it back on the nightstand and sat next to her hip on the mattress. He smiled. She tried for a smile in return.

"You look terrified, Abe." Her hand came up and cupped his chin.

He shrugged and forced a shaky hand through his hair. "The brick, and now this." Anger settled in the pit of his stomach. Someone was playing games.

"Am I being bullied?" She bit her bottom lip. "I'm sad to say that they succeeded."

His stomach twisted in knots. "I won't leave the house again."

"That's ludicrous." She waved a hand. "I appreciate the heroic gesture, but that's impossible. We have lives. We can't cut short our daily coming and goings because a lunatic is on the loose."

He buried his face in his palms. This was crazy. Willow Creek was the kind of town where people didn't need to lock their doors. Parents let their children play alone outdoors. Everyone lent a hand to help their neighbors. People didn't throw bricks through windows; not in these parts.

Until now.

Who would do such a thing? Who wanted Dee to leave town so badly they'd go to such extremes as breaking into his house? He couldn't think of one person.

"I'm okay," she said. "I'm tougher than I look."

He lowered his hands and looked at her. In the candlelight she looked like a child, scared and vulnerable. A spider web clung to her hair. She'd likely go berserk if she knew. He reached up and ran his hand down her long tresses, making sure to catch the web. She was none the wiser. "You're a brave trooper. I'm surprised you didn't break the door down."

"Thank goodness I didn't encounter any little critters while I was down there. It's unforgivable for a grown woman to pee herself."

"It would have been very unforgivable. I wet myself once when I was ten," he admitted.

"You were little. A lot of things are scary to kids."

"Like my own shadow?"

"What?"

"It was dark and I was coming out of the bathroom. I saw this black figure on the wall and then...whoosh." He swooped his hands. "It disappeared."

"Are you still afraid of your own shadow?"

"No, I'm good." He ran his palms down his legs. "I should go and check things outside, then call Sheriff Stansey."

Dee lowered her eyes to her folded hands. When she looked back up at him, her gaze pleaded. "Abe, please don't leave me."

With her long lashes, crystal blue eyes and puckered lower lip, she tore straight through him. He couldn't have left her side if his life depended on it. "I wouldn't for anything in the world," he answered.

He got up, removed his boots and shirt and climbed into bed beside her, atop the covers.

"Can I wear one of your shirts, Abe?"

"There are clean shirts in the middle drawer. Help yourself."

"No bother. I'll just wear this one." She stretched her body over him to reach the floor and pick up his discarded shirt. "It's all warm and smells like you." She brought it to her nose and inhaled.

Every nerve ending in his body tingled, alive. "I'm hoping it's a good smell, if you want to wear my clothes."

"Musk and soap." Her voice was breathy.

She pulled off her shirt. He respectfully closed his eyes, but only for a second. He took in her beauty as she undressed. The light played over her skin like liquid gold, drawing his eyes to caress the soft, slender arc of her back and the narrow curve of her waist. She unfastened her jeans and pushed them down her hips. He couldn't conceal his desire any longer. A deep moan vibrated his chest.

She flashed him a penetrating look.

Damn, he needed to reign himself in. "Should I apologize?"

"Only if you mean it." Her warm gaze fell to his bulging zipper.

He stayed quiet.

Pulling his shirt on, she climbed back under the covers. He kept his eyes on the ceiling. She reached over, ran a finger down the plain of his chest, along the plateau of his stomach, and stopped at the waist of his jeans. She hooked her finger into the material. "Wouldn't you be more comfortable out of these?" she asked.

"Probably," he answered, still keeping his eyes glued to the ceiling. Then she heaved a sigh.

"We're both adults, Abe. We've had sex. It's a little late to act shy with me. Feel free to take off your jeans. In fact, take everything else off, too. I'll promise I'll be good." She winked. "Very, very good."

She was teasing him. Someone had just threatened her life. He needed to control his desires and protect her. If he gave in to desire, need would leave his mind out of working order.

They were both safer with his jeans on, not to mention they hid an arousal that just wouldn't go down. "I'm comfortable. Thanks anyway."

"Are you playing hard to get?" she purred.

"We should get some sleep." he mumbled thickly. His resistance wavered by the second. The slender finger tucked into his waistband didn't help.

He started reciting the Pledge of Allegiance in his head. It didn't work. His cock remained hard and throbbing.

"I have a confession," she told him.

"This isn't a slumber party, so I don't need to know."

"I must."

"Unless it's to tell me that you kick, bite or punch in your sleep, keep it to yourself."

"I found the picture of you, me and Jacob you kept in the book."

He shrugged. "It's probably been there for years. I haven't been through any of those books for who knows how long." He counted the swirly designs on the ceiling.

"The book was pulled out, away from the others."

He swallowed hard. "A picture, huh?"

She slid closer to him, draping her bare thigh over his. "I thought it was sweet."

"You shouldn't."

"You're some piece of work." She sighed. "Can't you just admit that we have a connection, Abe?"

"If I say yes, you'll certainly use it against me."

"Fine." She slid back to her side of the bed and buried her head into her pillow. "I get the hint. I could take off all of my clothes and you still wouldn't flinch. You're a man of steel, Abe Matthew Delaney."

He rolled over, raising himself above her almost fast enough to make himself dizzy. He moved his face close to hers. "What do you want me to say? Do you want to hear how I'd lie awake every night thinking of you? Or should I tell you that when Jacob was home with you, I'd have to sleep in my office for fear I'd hear you laugh or moan because he'd touched you?" He shot a hand through his hair. "I wanted it to be me making you moan with desire. Shall I tell you I was so consumed with guilt for those thoughts, I planned to leave the farm?" He finally took a breath, and exhaled painfully. "He knew I cared for you, and you know what he told me?"

"No, I don't," she whispered. Her eyes filled with tears.

"He asked me to stay, not to leave, because he wanted me to take care of you." His voice clotted in his throat. He closed his eyes and fought for strength.

She touched his cheek with her warm palm. He opened his eyes and looked down at her. "Abe, you're not a bad person. You did nothing wrong. We haven't done anything wrong. Open the door and let me in."

He pulled back. "Why did Jacob stay away even more after that conversation?" The question had haunted him for years.

"He knew you'd take care of me."

"Was my brother truly that absorbed in his own issues?" he asked.

"Yes, he was." She sighed. Her breath swept across his cheek. "More than you know."

"Where do we go from here?" His eyes met hers. He found a solace there that washed over him like freedom.

"Wherever we want."

He threaded shaky fingers through her silken tresses and brought the strands to his nose. Coconut. He liked the scent, but it didn't help him forget the demons of the past. The straps of restraint loosened. All he needed to do was stretch, and they would be broken forever.

How could he deny himself bliss for another moment? Hadn't he paid his dues in guilt and anguish for the last five years?

She swept the pad of her finger along his lower lip. "Take me, Abe."

His control snapped.

His mouth descended on hers in a harsh release of pent-up passion and desire. She met his kiss fully, nipping his upper lip in a thrilling taunt. His mouth softened, but the urgency grew.

Skimming his hand slowly down her waist, along the slight curve of her hips, he glided his palm over the smooth, bare skin of her thigh. He slid his hand between her thighs, absorbing her heat. He pushed her panties off her hips, down the silky length of her legs, and slung them over the edge of the bed. His fingers delved into her delicate folds. She arched against him, opening wider, welcoming his stroke.

She caught him by surprise when she slid out from under him, then forced him back onto the mattress. He smiled as she kissed his bare chest, his stomach, working her way leisurely to the waist of his jeans. She nibbled, kissed and teased the sensitive skin around his navel until she finally unzipped his zipper and caressed his full, taut erection with a greedy touch.

The slide of her hand down his taut skin sent tingles through his veins. She was a sweet poison he couldn't resist and didn't want to He wanted to fall into the madness. He was lost and he didn't care.

* * * *

Dee glanced up at Abe through her lashes, watching his eyes turn a darker shade of brown. She wrapped her hand around the base of his erection, savoring the softness of his tight skin. She brought the tip of him into her mouth. He let out a tortured moan. He dug his fingers into her hair as she drew him in deeper, suckling him, closing the back of her throat around the round head. She tasted the creamy saltiness of him. His tense muscles made her wonder if he could last much longer.

He moved. She protested with a moan. He lifted her up and drew her on top of him, her legs straddling his hips. "I wasn't finished," she said.

"But I almost was," he replied through a heavy breath. She rolled her hips across his cock. Her wetness made him slick.

He lifted up, gently laid her on the comforter and made haste in removing his jeans. His fingers roughly brushed her flesh as he unfastened the clasp, skimmed along her ribs and barely grazed her breasts as he lifted the flimsy fabric away. He pulled her shirt up, trapping her arms above her head. The feeling of being exposed before him, vulnerable, was exciting.

The anticipation of what came next caused her breathing to grow heavy. When he didn't thrust into her, she glanced up at him. He held back, stroking her with a needy gaze. "You're so damn beautiful, Dee." He plucked a pearly pink nipple between two fingers. "I'm going to taste you."

He dipped between her thighs. He kissed just above her pubic bone, then found her cleft with his forefinger, parting her nether lips. His tongue flicked out and licked her clit. He sampled her like a fine wine.

Fire burned her insides like molten lava. She needed him to take her, claim her, satisfy her need. She dug her fingers into his back, raking him with her nails as she tugged at him.

He lifted up on his knees and rubbed his moist chin with the back of his hand. His eyes were bright, glistening, dragging her in.

She watched as he reached into the nightstand and pulled out a small package. He tore the paper off the condom and rolled the latex down his erection. He lifted himself between her knees. She spread her thighs, readying herself for him.

He teased her with his member, circling her entrance, entering partway, then withdrawing. She lifted to meet him, splaying her hands across his ass, digging her fingers into his skin. He flexed, and his muscles tightened. She pulled him and he followed, burying himself inside her.

Dee thought she could lose her soul. Their connection seemed right. It was dangerous for anyone to feel this good, this complete. An explosion flooded their bodies as they thrust and clung to one another.

He rolled over and tugged her against his side. She laid her head against his chest, listening to the strong rhythm of his heart. It matched the beat of hers as she fell into a deep, peaceful sleep.

* * * *

The next morning Dee woke, stretched languidly and smiled. The night with Abe had been gloriously satisfying. She could never have imagined lovemaking being more consuming. Her inner thighs tingled.

Dee snuggled under the blankets, closed her eyes and sighed lazily. She didn't want the feeling to ever end. She wanted to lie here forever, to soak up the warm memories that surrounded her in bliss. Rolling over, she reached out to wrap an arm around Abe.

He was gone.

The bedroom door opened and closed with a soft *click*. She lifted herself up. Abe stood beside the bed with two steaming cups in his hand. He held one out for her. "Coffee?"

"Mmm." She leaned against the wooden headboard, allowing the sheet to fall casually around her chest, revealing her bare breasts. He swept his gaze over her nudity. Her nipples roused with a tingle, erect and inviting his touch. He winced and her stomach dropped. She jerked the cover back up.

From the look on his face, she wouldn't like what he was about to say.

He sat on the side of the bed. "Good morning."

She arched a brow. "Dark circles, frown, tell-tale crinkle between your eyes...hmm, I don't think it's such a good morning. I didn't even get a kiss."

One corner of his mouth quirked, a smile that fizzled before it reached his eyes. "I'm sorry." He bent forward and kissed her briefly on the lips.

Her heart sank. If he didn't want to repeat the night before, he could have at least kissed her properly. Passionately. Not that cold, brief peck.

She set her untouched cup on the night table and pushed back the covers. When she started to get up, he laid a hand on her arm. She looked at him and said, "I'm getting up."

"We need to talk." He set his cup next to hers.

The temperature dropped from chilly to frozen in a matter of seconds. "I don't like that look, Abe." She swallowed past the constriction in her throat. "You're scaring me."

"I was up before dawn, doing some investigating. I found the electrical wires cut on the outside box. I also found footprints along the edge of the woods, and near the fence."

She wrapped her arms tightly around her waist. "Then I was right. Someone was in here with me, and locked the door to the basement." She paused. "I'll call Sheriff Stansey."

He shook his head. "I already called, and he's come and gone."

"Does he still think this is the case of a couple of bored teens?"

"He doesn't know what to think." His brow furrowed. "Could you have made an enemy back in Chicago, and they followed you here? Or, was there a man..."

"Stop, Abe." She threw her head back and lifted her chin. "I have no enemies. There was no man."

"I'll stay with you. Stansey said he'd send a deputy out to check on the place a couple of times a day."

"So, basically, I'll live in a guarded prison?" She climbed out of bed. Feeling Abe's gaze on her, she began looking for her clothes. Although any other time she would have been comfortable standing before him nude, right now she felt vulnerable. She grabbed the first thing she came to and pulled it on. It was his shirt from last night. It hung past her hips.

"No, Dee--"

"Good, because I refuse to live that way."

He sighed and squeezed the bridge of his nose between his thumb and forefinger. "There is another option."

She paused. "Another option?" Then it came to her, as clear as the morning light. "Oh. That option." He wanted her to leave.

He stood up and moved toward her. "Let me explain."

He reached out to touch her. She dodged. "Go on, Abe. Say it! Tell me the details of this plan you've cooked up."

"It would only be until we found out who's doing this to you."

She wanted to laugh and cry at the same time. Tears won out. "Boy, this works out for you, doesn't it?"

"How, Dee?" He clenched his hands into fists. "You think I want you to go back to Chicago? I don't want you to leave, but your life may be in danger here. What if I can't keep you safe?"

"It's not your responsibility to keep me safe. I've been taking care of myself just fine all these years."

"Just like you took care of yourself last night?"

Anger shot through her. That was a low blow. "I should have known you'd find a way to push me out the door again."

"That's not fair."

"It isn't? Maybe this--this maniac knows how much you want me gone, and is doing your dirty work for you. Maybe it's someone who wants you to be happy." She was being irrational. She knew it. She just didn't care. Her heart was breaking.

His body tensed and his jaw tightened. "Hell, Dee. Listen to yourself."

The previous night's warmth and passion vanished. They'd been so close, so intimate, and now it was all gone, or buried beneath fear and anguish. They'd both drawn a line, and she'd stepped over it.

"It didn't have to be this way." Disappointment edged Abe's voice.

"No, it didn't. I could have walked away quietly." She sniffed back a tear.

"Before the accusations started." He turned away from her, placing both palms on the dresser. "I'm glad you have such a high opinion of me."

A sob bubbled up in her throat. She pushed it back. "I should have known better than to think last night would change anything. I guess I should have seen this one coming." Her voice quavered, but she stiffened her spine. She could at least walk out with her pride. She glared at his back, practically slicing between his shoulder blades, but he wouldn't turn or look at her. Fine. Let it be that way.

She walked out, defeat a heavy burden on her shoulders. Her own room offered little refuge. Pain racked her body. Part of her wanted to turn back around, go down the hall and force Abe to listen. Didn't he realize the farm was her home? Leaving meant breaking her heart in two.

But he didn't care about that. He didn't want her here, and that was that.

With tears misting her eyes, she grabbed an overnight bag and began throwing clothes in. Once it was full, she closed it. The rest of her things could stay here.

When she ventured downstairs, Abe was nowhere in sight. Good. Dee didn't want to see him. If he spoke to her, she might break down.

But if he thought she'd run away to Chicago, he had another thing coming.

Chapter 14

Not much had changed, Dee thought as she strolled through the front door of O'Malley's, Willow Creek's historical watering hole. She'd left the farm two days ago, and had stayed with Lita since. Abe hadn't called or attempted to speak to her. George had invited her for a beer, and she'd accepted.

As she stepped into the room, Dee felt a sense of déjà vu. The low-lit room smelled of brisket and kraut--the O'Malley's specialty--and strong ale. The hardworking patrons loved to chat with their neighbors while warming their stomachs with whiskey. The jukebox, the only modern piece of equipment, looked out of place. A slow country song played, about a man getting his truck vandalized.

The walls were obscured by the memorabilia and knick-knacks George had collected over the years. There were funny pictures of drunken patrons, old shot glasses and a huge framed portrait of Dudley O'Malley hanging proudly above the bottles of booze.

George popped his head up from behind the bar and bellowed, "The cat went and caught himself a ray of sunshine. Look at that, boys!" He tossed her a wink.

Ten pairs of eyes stared at her. Familiar faces looked up at her in curiosity. Among them were Dusty and Tate Johnson, Marshall Cox, one of the more faithful patrons, and a few others.

The Johnson twins greeted her with a friendly smile and a salute from their longneck bottles. She awkwardly waved back. She knew the boys, but only through rumor. The only thing they liked more than drinking was women.

"You still treating this place like your baby, George?" Dee asked.

"What more could a proud father ask for?" He wiggled his brows.

She smiled as she found a table in the far corner and sat in a wooden chair that had seen better days. A few minutes later George came over with a mug of beer, just as the music changed. This time a woman sang about her cheating husband and how she'd tossed him out on his ear, but not before she'd spent all his money on a new wardrobe and a diamond ring.

"Should I have brought a glass of wine?" George asked.

She gave him a flippant smile. "Beer's fine, George."

"Glad you decided to stop in."

Dee remembered the last time she'd been in the pub. She'd sat at the bar, crying into her beer while George listened like a true bartender and friend. Jacob had just died, and Abe was distant. Her world had seemed to fall apart that day. "Do you forgive me for being gone so long?"

He sighed. "Only if I get a kiss."

Getting up, she stood on tiptoes and gave him a quick kiss on the cheek. He burst into laughter, reached out and grabbed her up, sweeping her off her feet.

"Not so fast there, big man." She pushed away and waved a finger in his face. "You're engaged, so you can't be seen hugging on other women," she teased.

"Well, well, well... You're as saucy as ever, aren't you, girl?"

"Come on, George!" one of the Johnson boys yelled from the bar, holding up an empty bottle.

"Okay, Tate. Keep your panties on." He turned back to Dee. "I'm the only one working the bar. The gal I had working for me up and quit last month. Good help is hard to find in these parts. Sorry I can't stay and chat."

"I forgive you."

"Are you gonna leave us again without even saying goodbye?" he asked.

"I will say goodbye if I plan to leave, I promise--but I plan to stay." She sat back down at the table as George walked away. "Hey George, is there any chance Abe will be in tonight?"

"Tonight's Tuesday..." He tugged at his ear. "No, I doubt it. Abe doesn't come in very often anymore. Are you two feuding again?"

She didn't answer.

"Now that's a familiar look." George returned to her table and pulled out a chair, ignoring the noisy boys at the bar. "The last time I saw that look, you were hanging your head over a mug of beer and mumbling something about Abe losing his sign. Two days later you bounced right out of town."

She slitted her eyes at him and bit back laughter. "I didn't say anything about Abe losing a sign. I told you Abe had lost his mind."

He grimaced. "You mean all these years I thought you were upset because Abe had lost a sign? No wonder he had looked at me like I was an idiot when I asked about it."

She eyed him, but decided not to ask. "George, what if I told you someone wanted me gone from this town?"

"I'd say Abe's bark is much bigger than his bite."

"Not Abe," she said. "Someone else."

He shrugged. "In this town, we welcome strangers so we have something or someone to talk about. The news of the Donahue's divorce is penny change now."

"Someone wants me gone enough that they'd be willing to scare me. I had a brick thrown through my bedroom window and someone cut electrical wires," she whispered.

"How about a beer over here!" one of the patrons shouted, slamming his fist on the bar.

"Yeah, yeah. I told you to keep your skirts on, boys," George yelled back.

"Go on, George. I know what happens when these men don't get their beer."

"All right, but we'll talk."

"I'll be here." She waved him off.

From her seat, she watched as Tate Johnson slid off his barstool, carrying two beers. It didn't take much to guess his intentions. She wasn't into the party scene--or him, for that matter--but if she wanted to find out details about people living in town she'd have to be friendly.

Tate drew closer, a cocky smile spreading over his features. He wasn't a bad-looking guy; in fact, he was handsome. He was younger than she. She guessed he was about twenty-five, with the swagger that said he thought his good looks could break any woman's heart. She suppressed a snicker. Did he actually think his boyish charm could work on her? What a titanic waste of time.

"Dee Crawford." His gaze trailed over her in admiration.

"Tate Johnson," she replied.

"I thought you might be ready for another." He set one of the beers down in front of her.

"I haven't touched the first yet."

He shrugged. "Can I sit?"

At least he'd asked. "Sure." She used her foot to push out the chair opposite her. The farther, the better.

"You looked a little lonely sitting over here in this dark corner." He took a long drink, keeping his eyes on her. "I was at your party, you know."

She nodded. "I remember. You were with a pretty brunette. You two seemed close." If by *close* she meant *all over each other.*

He laughed. "That was Silvia. I met her a few months ago at the racetrack. There's nothing serious between us."

"You're still racing cars?" she asked.

He nodded. "You bet."

"Does your brother still race?" Dee glanced over at Dusty, who still nursed his beer.

Tate shot his brother a gloomy look. "He's sulking. His wife left him, and they're getting a divorce."

A twinge of empathy made Dee wince. "Molly?" She and Jacob had gone to the couple's wedding. Molly had seemed very sweet and quiet.

"Yeah, pretty lame, huh?"

She nodded. Her gaze lingered on Dusty. He was just another reminder that things changed, people changed...and it was far too easy to feel left behind.

"What about you, Dee? Where have you been hiding out these last few years?"

"Interesting choice of words, hiding out." She sat back in her chair and eyed him coolly.

"Okay, where did you go?"

"I moved in with my mom," she replied.

He laughed dryly. "Yeah? I still live with my mom, too. Look, how about a shot? Sounds like we could both use one." He flagged George's attention and called for two tequilas.

Dee smiled. Tate was harmless, and not bad company. Though, after two more rounds of shots, his charm was a little more effective. Maybe because she was woozy. She wasn't sure if it was the tequila or Tate's non-stop chatter about racecars, women and an old windmill on his property.

"How about some music, Tate?" She rummaged through her purse and found some quarters buried at the bottom, along with an old piece of gum, a wad of paper, a tube of lipstick and a hairpin. She tossed all of it onto the table. The items scattered across the waxed wood. "Do you like to dance?" she asked.

"Um..."

"Did the cat get your tongue? It's a yes or no question." She slid out of her chair, caught his hand, dragged him from his seat and led him toward the floor. "Will you dance with me, Tate Johnson?"

He shrugged and followed her out to the small parquet floor, worn from years and years of dancing. She dropped a couple of quarters into the jukebox, punched in some random choices and listened as a familiar tune filled the room. "I love this song." She slid up next to a bewildered Tate and swirled her hips.

Nervously, he said, "I'm not a very good dancer." He took a cautious step back.

"Oh, pfft. You move fine. You've just got to loosen up a little." She grabbed his slender hips. "Just relax your hips and arms." She guided him in circular motions, turning and twisting. "How about another tequila?" She laughed loudly. "Hey, George, send us another round." She was feeling good.

George looked at her and shook his head.

"Oh come on, George, why be a party pooper?"

"You've had enough," he shouted over the loud music.

"What's wrong with him, Tate? We could use another round, couldn't we?" She swayed to the music, but Tate stood statue-still.

"I think we're finished." His voice cracked.

"What are you rambling about? I'm just getting started." She looked up at him in confusion. His face turned pale and he looked a little green around the edges. He stared at something over her shoulder. "What is it? Are you going to be sick?" She followed his gaze.

Leaning against the jukebox was none other than Abe. His tall, muscular frame seemed exceptionally large in the small area. All laughter deserted her, leaving her a little dizzy.

He uncrossed his booted feet and pushed toward her. Their eyes locked, unwavering. "What are you doing here?" she snapped, more harshly than she'd intended.

He held her eyes as he drew closer, stopping a few feet away. "This is a public place, Dee," he mocked, eyes narrowed.

"But is it coincidence you happened to show up the one evening I'm here?" she retorted. A wave of dizziness swept over her, and she lost her balance. She fell back into the chest of a very quiet, very still Tate Johnson.

Abe's jaw tightened and his eyes turned to ice, practically shredding poor Tate. Tate steadied her and quickly removed his hands from her body.

Abe said, "George can't babysit you when he needs to worry about his other patrons."

She shot George a razor-sharp glare. Why that... Had he called Abe to "rescue" her? George shrugged and mouthed an apology. She growled. "Why did he call you? Needed another party pooper to kill the mood?"

"It's time to go home," Abe said through thin lips. The vein in his forehead grew thicker by the second.

"I'm not going anywhere. I'm dancing," she slurred, and cringed at her own voice.

"With whom?" He raised an eyebrow

"With Tate." She turned to an empty dance floor. Tate sat at the bar next to his brother, his head down. "Oh, that's great. Just hunky-dory."

She heard a coin clink as it dropped into the jukebox. She whirled back around to find Abe punching in a song code. When he turned to her, he said softly, "You want to dance, we'll dance. After all, I didn't get one at your party."

Dee's mouth fell open, but the words never surfaced. The slow song was a familiar one, made for lovers. He took her hand and pulled her gently into his arms.

She reached up and wrapped her arms around his neck. "Don't think this will change anything."

"It changes everything," he whispered into her ear.

"For whom?" Her mind screamed at her to pull back, but she wanted to be near him far too much--needed *him* far too much.

"For the both of us."

"How?"

"Because I--" He stopped and rubbed his eyes. "It just does."

"I didn't need you to come here and rescue me, Abe." She kept her eyes on everything but him. His look drilled into her, intense and intensely uncomfortable.

"You had everything under control. My suggestion is, don't give up baking to teach dance lessons."

She scoffed. "So you've lowered yourself once again to spying on me?" she accused.

"Not exactly. You're just too damn drunk to realize I came in and sat down almost three songs ago." He pushed a tendril of hair away from her face. "I think Tate thought he was going to get lucky tonight."

Although her heart stung like it was ripping in two, she didn't falter. The second she let herself need him, it would be open season on pain. "He just may have if you hadn't come along."

Once the words left her lips, she wanted to snatch them back. She'd gone too far. He withdrew his hand from her back and carefully pushed her away. "We're leaving now," he commanded.

"Wait." She dug in her heels. "I owe George for my tab."

"Hey George, we'll settle tomorrow," Abe shouted over his shoulder as he took Dee by the hand and led her out the door.

She could have fought him, but it wouldn't have done any good. He'd have carried her out caveman-style if necessary, and only embarrassed her more.

Once they were outside and out of sight of staring eyes, she jerked her hand from his and folded her arms under her breasts. "Okay, stop!"

He turned to her, eyes narrowed and gaze as sharp as ice picks. "What the hell is the matter with you?"

She exhaled. "What's wrong with me? I should be asking what's wrong with you. How dare you treat me like you own me? I'm an adult, well over the age of twenty-one, and if I want to hang out at O'Malley's and dance all night, I have that privilege."

"You're wasted," he snarled.

"Bingo, you're a genius."

"We're leaving. Get in the truck."

"Hell no."

* * * *

Abe buried his face in his palms and counted to ten. Everyone had the right to get drunk once in a while. Sure. They could even act like drunk jackasses. It was usually pretty funny, but there was nothing funny about a midnight call from George O'Malley, telling him Dee was wasted and headed for trouble. He'd been ready to deal with her attitude. He'd known she wouldn't want to leave with him. What he hadn't expected was finding her cozied up with one of the biggest womanizers in the county.

When she'd touched Johnson, it had ripped through Abe like a bolt of lightning. He'd wanted to jump up and tear Tate's head off just for standing next to her, but he'd learned over the years that fighting was never the answer. It only resulted in black eyes and bloody noses, not resolutions. He didn't like another man touching Dee, but he also realized she wasn't interested in the Johnson kid. He knew the signs of her desire. He should. She'd nearly burnt him alive with her passion.

"You're too drunk to drive, Dee. Be reasonable."

"I don't plan to drive. I'll sit in my car all night, or I'll walk."

"You're acting like a child. You know you're not going to sleep in your car, and it's too far to walk to Lita's." He breathed in and out sharply. "Get it through your head. You're leaving with me."

"I bet Tate will give me a ride home."

Before the words were even finished, he'd crossed the gravel lot and pulled her roughly against the hard wall of his chest. "Like he's any more safe to drive."

"Are you jealous?" she asked.

"Not in the slightest. You have no interest in him," he said.

"And how can you be so sure?"

"Because the only time I've ever seen desire in your eyes is when you're looking at me." He pulled her harder against his body.

"You don't know what you're talking about," she snapped.

"When you're turned on, your eyes turn the darkest blue, your lips pucker ever so slightly, and your cheeks get flushed. No, I didn't even see a mere sign of passion while you were dancing with Tate." He lowered his voice. "I'm seeing that look right now."

She screwed up her face as if trying to force it to obey. "What you're talking about is just the sign of a woman in heat. Yet we've had sex, and it left me cold."

He pressed his lips against hers, sliding his tongue into her mouth. She succumbed and melted against him. She wrapped her arms around his shoulders and dug her fingers deep into his skin. The thin layer of his shirt hardly barred the heat of her touch. He found the hem of her shirt and delved inside to touch the warm skin of her flat stomach. He lifted her body closer to his, so close the apex of her thighs rested against the hardness behind his zipper.

"Abe..." His name floated from her lips on the wings of a whisper.

"Do I leave you cold, baby?" He was breathless.

"No, Abe."

"Tell me. Tell me what you want, sweetheart."

"I want you, Abe. It's always been you."

Abe gave her one last kiss before pulling away, leaving coldness between them. "You're lucky, sweetheart, because I'd like to take you right here and now, but 'sloppy drunk' isn't my taste. I want you to remember every feeling, every emotion when we make love again." He then turned on his heel and headed to the driver's side of the truck.

"I'm not getting in your truck!" she flung at his back.

"Get in the truck."

"Let's take the Jeep." She pulled her key from her front pocket.

"No, my truck."

She climbed into the passenger side of his truck. "Oh, no. My purse? Did you grab it?"

"No. I'll go back and get it." Damned if he'd let her out of the truck after it took so long to get her in.

Abe headed back into the bar. Tate Johnson avoided his eyes as he checked Dee's table. No sign of her purse; nor had George seen it. Abe made it back out to the parking lot just in time to watch Dee lean out the truck and toss her cookies, leaving a trail down the passenger-side door.

He groaned, waited until she was finished, then said, "You win. We'll take the Jeep."

She slid out of the truck and gave him an apologetic look. "I'm sorry, Abe. I do feel much better, though."

"Good." He opened the Jeep's passenger-side door and helped her in. "I'd suggest sitting there with the door open for a minute."

"Why?"

"Because there's a good chance you'll be sick again."

"How do you know?" she asked, pulling back her long hair.

"Your purse is missing."

He was right. She threw up again.

Once she finished, he buckled her in and took the driver's seat. They'd barely pulled out of the parking lot before the sky opened and rain pelted down. Abe could hardly see through the windshield, even with the wipers on full blast. He glanced over at Dee. She rested her head against the window, her eyes closed. After vomiting the second time, she seemed to have gotten it all out of her system, was feeling better...and was quiet. Almost too quiet. His anger had subsided as well.

How could he stay angry with her?

Chapter 15

Dee woke to the sound of gravel underneath the tires. She glanced across the seat at Abe, who stared at her with a strange expression. "Are you upset with me?" She slumped her shoulders.

He shook his head. "I should be, but for some reason I'm not."

"It's pouring outside."

"We could sit here for a few minutes and wait for it to slow down, unless you need to hit the bathroom."

"I'm fine. What do you think happened to my purse?" Her stomach twisted.

He shrugged and smacked the heel of his hand against the steering wheel. "I don't know. I was only there for a short while, so someone must have taken it while we were arguing."

She pressed her fingers against her head. "Maybe someone who was sitting at the bar?"

He hesitated, then said, "I can't be one hundred percent positive, but if I had to guess I'd say no. The Johnson boys are known to be rowdy, but not thieves. The rest of the crowd is harmless. I asked George if he saw anyone take it, but he said he didn't. I'll talk to him later."

The rain had slowed. "Well, this may be our chance to get inside. The rain has died down some."

They both jumped out of the Jeep and ran to the front door. The rain had almost stopped, but they were still soaked by the time they reached the porch, breathing as hard as if they'd run a mile. Dee's hair matted to her head, and her clothes were drenched. His gaze dropped to her chest, drawing her eyes down. The cotton shirt she wore did nothing to conceal her bra, or her erect nipples underneath it.

"Are you cold?" he asked.

"No." She trembled from his nearness, but not the weather. He looked at her differently, and she didn't know why. He bent his head to kiss her eyelids, the tip of her nose and her cheeks.

Reaching down, he started to lift her into his arms when they were struck by headlights coming up the drive. He froze. She jumped from his grip, moving away from him.

The truck came closer. Dee realized it was Abe's neighbor, Vicky Donahue.

Vicki climbed from the pickup. "I'm sorry. I tried to call, but there was no answer. My mare's about to foal, and I can't reach the vet. I need help."

"I'll be right behind you," Abe assured her.

"I want to come. Maybe I can be of some use?" Dee asked, her bottom lip trembling more now. Abe raised a brow, looking at her. She shrugged. "There may be something."

"You shouldn't be alone, anyway. Go get some dry clothes on."

Dee ran so fast that she almost stumbled on the stairs. She got to her room, threw off her wet clothes and quickly tossed on dry ones. She stopped in the bathroom, brushed her teeth and got halfway down the stairs when she remembered something. She rushed back up the stairs to Abe's room and grabbed him a dry shirt.

By the time she made it outside, Abe was waiting for her in the Jeep. She climbed into the seat beside him. Dee held out the shirt. When he blinked quizzically, she said, "I thought you might like a dry shirt."

"I will, but there's no need to change now. I'll wait till after the mess."

In the time it took to get to the Donahues' barn, a few miles up the road, the storm stopped. All that remained was the faint rumble of thunder as it moved on.

The barn was dark, barely lit by a dim lamp hung far back in one of the stalls. As they drew closer, Dee saw the mare lying on her side. Vicky crouched nearby, talking in a whisper-soft voice. "It's okay, girl, you'll be fine."

"It's so dark. Will you be able to see?" The question was meant for Abe, but Vicky answered.

"The bright light irritates her."

"Have you already cleaned her up?" Abe asked as he examined the mare.

"Scrubbed and ready."

"You know, Vicky, I'm not the best candidate to do this. I've only helped foal twice." Concern drew lines around Abe's mouth and eyes.

"I left Doc Steward a message and told her. That was an hour ago." She smiled. "I trust you'll do fine."

The mare was visibly uncomfortable. Her sides, matted with sweat, heaved in rapid pants. Her chocolate eyes were distant and glazed. Dee watched in fascination. She'd never seen a baby's birth before. Sure, it wasn't human, but that didn't matter. New life was miraculous.

"How long will it take?" Dee asked. Curiosity bubbled inside her.

"It can take ten minutes, or an hour." Abe shrugged, stretching his white, still-damp shirt across his back. "It goes pretty smoothly unless there's a problem."

The words were barely out when the mare let out a peculiar sound. A yellowish fluid gushed from between her legs, covering the hay-strewn floor.

"Is that, uhh, normal?" Dee said, pointing at the puddle.

"It's called amniotic fluid." Abe turned to Vicky and said, "Doc will want to know that it's tinged yellow. Foal's probably just stressed and discharging." Josephine let out another high-pitched wail. Abe bent lower to examine her. "I think we're ready."

"Doing good, Josephine," Vicky soothed. "Let it happen, girl."

A white sac protruded from the horse's backside, easing ever slowly outward, but then stopped and slid back inside. Abe cursed and glanced at Vicky. "I think we have a problem."

Vicky stepped around and dropped to her knees. Abe laid a hand on her shoulder. "I'll do it. Besides, my arm is longer and stronger. You keep her calm." The mare grunted and stretched her neck. "Damn!" Abe murmured.

Abe knelt on the floor, armpit deep in the horse, and attempted to wriggle the foal free. She knew then why he hadn't changed his shirt, and what'd he'd meant by a mess. A loud pop pierced the quiet barn. Abe quickly moved away.

"The foal's foot was stuck," he explained.

Dee stepped back from the stall until she felt wood scratch her back. She heard a sniff and turned. A large horse rested its nose on her shoulder. Dee squealed and jumped so high that she tripped and landed on her knees.

Abe looked over at her. Dee stared back, positioned on all fours, her backside sticking ungracefully into the air. He chuckled. "Are you okay?"

"I...I'm fine."

"He just wanted to check you out." Vicky offered with a wink and smile.

Josephine made another deep sound, drawing every eye back to her. The bluish-white pouch emerged again, sliding down swiftly. Dee stood, dusted herself off, watching mesmerized as the foal's head came, and then the entire body.

Abe and Vicky moved rapidly, ripping open the sac, then removing the obstructions from the foal's mouth and nose. The foal looked up and seemed to catch Dee's eyes. Warm, interested brown. Joy swelled inside of Dee.

Once the foal moved its hooves, Josephine swung around to check out what was making the commotion. The mare paused in her examination, sniffing the slimy creature lying at her side, then ran her muzzle along his neck. Josephine snorted; the foal responded with a low, whimpering nicker

Tears streamed down Dee's face. When she felt Abe's eyes on her, she swiped the moisture on her face. "I'll meet you outside," she said, and bolted almost before the words fell from her lips.

Dee waited in the Jeep. She couldn't seem to stop quivering. She couldn't blame it all on the birth of the foal. Abe had saved the foal's life. She had even seen the mist of unshed tears in his eyes when the foal was born. If she hadn't already realized how crazy in love she was with the man, she would have fallen head over heels at that very moment. And if Vicky hadn't interrupted them on the porch earlier, she and Abe would have ended up in bed, doing more than just talking. The thought made her melt back into the seat in a puddle of desire. She wanted him so deeply.

Something had to change. She couldn't imagine life without him, but sure as heck couldn't imagine life with him. Not with the way they argued.

She looked out the window, into the darkness, and sighed. Her eyes soon closed and she drifted into a deep sleep.

* * * *

An hour later, Abe climbed in beside Dee. She was sound asleep. He smiled. It had taken him a while, helping with the foal and cleaning up afterward. He had washed up and changed into the shirt Dee had grabbed for him.

He reached out, touched a long tendril of her hair and wrapped it around his finger. She'd been affected by tonight's miracle birth. He'd seen it in her eyes.

She stirred. Her eyes fluttered open. She offered him a sweet, innocent smile. "Hi." Her voice was hoarse from sleep.

"Hi." Abe moved his finger down her smooth cheek. "Sorry it took so long."

She rolled her head across the headrest. "No apology necessary. It was amazing, Abe." The security light flowed through the window, reflecting in her eyes like diamonds.

"Yes, it was," he said.

"Is the foal all right?"

"He's fine. How about you? Head spinning?"

"No, I feel fine."

He swept his touch along the slight curve of her bottom lip. "Come home with me?"

There was no hesitation when she answered, "Yes."

He started the Jeep and pulled out, heading toward the farm.

* * * *

The next morning, Abe returned to the bedroom just as Dee rolled over in bed. She moaned and brought a hand to her temple. Yeah, just as he'd thought. She had a hangover.

Her eyes fluttered open and she turned her head. "My head is throbbing."

Abe bit back a chuckle and instead offered a bottle of aspirin and a steaming cup of coffee. "I thought you might need a caffeine fix and a pain reliever."

"You're a man of all men." She took the mug from him.

Abe popped the lid, emptied two pills into his palm and handed them to her. "You look like you've been to hell and back." Her hair stood on end, and her eyeliner smeared a black trail around her eyes. She was still the sexiest woman he'd ever seen.

"Thanks. I appreciate your insults." She grabbed the aspirin and swallowed them. "Point is, I don't even care."

She buried her face into her hand and rubbed her forehead with the tips of her fingers. He wanted to be hard on her after last night, but didn't have it in him. They'd made up when they got home. Although they'd had a PG-13 evening, with a little kissing and petting, he hadn't tried for anything more. She had been tired and still coming down from her bender. He'd held her until she fell asleep.

"I had a feeling you'd wake up feeling pretty lousy, so I thought I'd better make the old standby."

She peered at him through parted fingers. He went to the dresser, grabbed a glass and held it up.

"What is this?" Her nose wrinkled.

"Family secret for hangovers." He set it before her.

She picked it up, took a whiff and pulled back with a sour look. "It smells hideous. What's in it?"

He shook his head. "I'm not sure if you're up for the ingredients."

She took a sip. Not a second later, her eyes widened. "That's spicy. What is it?"

"Tomato juice, hot sauce, a shot of vodka, and the real surprise... anchovies," he said. She wrinkled her nose and stuck out her tongue. He laughed. "I promise, you'll feel better after you drink it. It's tried, true and tested. And I have some good news for you." He sat on the end of the bed.

"Really?"

"Well actually, two good things." He laid a hand on her blanket-covered foot. "First, I heard from Vicky. She wanted us to be the first to know that she named the foal Dee."

Her eyes rounded. "She named the horse after me?"

"Vicky said she tried your cookies and lemon pie at the party, and they were the best she'd ever had. She hoped she could butter you up."

"Butter me up?"

"For the recipes."

"I'm flattered...I guess. I've never had a horse, or any animal, named after me."

"Better news...Stansey got a call from a county worker who picks up trash along the roadway. He found your purse in the ditch. He turned it over. Stansey said it appears everything was still in it--driver's license, credit cards, and legal papers. And get this, all your money was still there. Did you have anything else?"

"I had the keys to the front door. I hadn't put them on the keychain yet. I'm glad my purse was found, but did the person who stole it intentionally take my keys, or were they lost along the road?"

Abe smoothed his hand over his hair. He'd asked himself the same question, but didn't want to worry her. She hesitated in drinking the concoction. He shook his head. "There are consequences to a night of tossing back tequila. You choose between a headache or a glass of my miracle cure. I'd suggest you drink it all."

She took another sip. "Can I go pick my purse up?"

"Stansey said he'd bring it out. He's having it dusted for prints. He wants to have a word with you about O'Malley's. He plans on stopping in and talking to all the patrons who were there last night."

"Someone had to see something."

"They were too busy watching us...or, shall I say, you." He could barely keep his eyes off her last night. When George had called him, he'd wasted no time in getting to her. She'd been like a breath of fresh air, even if he'd wanted to bend her over his knee.

"Abe, you've lived in this town your whole life. Do you have a clue who could be doing all of these crazy things?"

"Town resident, yes. Detective, no." Or he'd be paying the son of a bitch a visit and introducing him to his knuckles. "I think someone followed you from Lita's into O'Malley's. You don't remember seeing anything out of the ordinary?"

"No, I didn't. All the men at the bar were harmless."

"Yeah, I bet. Tate didn't look harmless. The man is a walking hard-on."

She rolled her eyes. "That doesn't make him dangerous."

He laughed.

"You know, I had my reasons for going into O'Malley's."

"What was it? To get liquored up?" he teased.

"No. I thought if I hung out long enough, I could find some answers. Someone has to know something. People talk and brag, especially when they hate another person and have a few too many beers."

"I don't think this person harassing you hates you, Dee."

"Then why stalk me?"

"If this person really wanted you gone forever, he would have harmed you a long time ago. He wants you to leave town. Who has motive for wanting you gone from Willow Creek?"

"You're assuming it's a man?"

"Don't you think so?"

"It could be a woman." She hesitated. "Do you think Melissa could be capable of doing this?"

He exhaled. "What would be her motive?"

She laughed. "Are you serious?"

He shrugged. "Melissa realizes she has no future with me. It has nothing to do with you being in Willow Creek or not."

Dee nodded. "In all honesty, I don't think it's her either. Mrs. Graves did cross my mind--until we buried the hatchet the other day."

He laughed. "Now that's funny."

"Why is that amusing?"

"Do I need to even answer that?"

"Okay, okay." Her shoulders slumped. "Then we're at a complete loss."

"You feel better?" He glanced down at the half-empty glass.

"Actually, I feel great."

"Then I'll take a thank you." He gently squeezed her toes.

She smiled. "Thank you. I do appreciate your help."

"Can I ask--do you plan on hanging out at O'Malley's every night, getting drunk in the name of investigation?" He held her eyes.

Her cheeks flushed. "No, I won't be doing that."

"Good. I'm not sure I can take many more midnight runs, not to mention protecting you from every horny man in the pub."

"You'll never let me live it down, will you?"

"It's already forgotten."

He'd forget anything she asked, just to have her on the farm.

Chapter 16

Dee stared down into her coffee, as if the answers to her problems would magically appear. She was glad to be back, but it hadn't solved the problem of their mistrust and arguing. They were like two magnets pushing against one another when all they needed was to let fate take its natural progression. With their history, sometimes letting go was easier said than done.

"I'm glad to be home, Abe. But I was hurt. If I'd stayed we would have ended up arguing, and more than likely saying things we'd regret."

He studied the pictures on the wall. "I think I've figured out a way to solve everything."

Was he leaving? Had he figured out a foolproof way to divide the farm evenly? She hoped to share it with him. She wanted it to be her home, too. "What is it?"

"Let's get married."

She almost fell out of bed. She wouldn't have been more shocked if he'd reached out and slapped her. She stared at him. "I must still be hung over. I thought I heard you say..." The word wouldn't even form on her tongue.

"Marriage. I suggested marriage."

She nodded jerkily. "Yes, that's what I thought I heard." She gulped.

"Dee, your hearing is fine." His gaze seemed to caress her. "I know it may seem abrupt, but I think it's the right thing to do."

"Abrupt? I'd say it's downright...well, preposterous." The sting of her fingernails digging into her palms made her unfold her hands. She ran them down her legs and laid them on her knees to stop their shaking. "Just a few days ago you sent me packing, and now you've done a complete turnaround. Pardon me if I don't transition that quickly."

"If you'll think it over, you'll see that marriage is a good thing."

"What's the selling point?" There was no denying that she had deep feelings for Abe. If she examined them closer, she knew she'd find she'd been in love with him for five years. But what would he gain? She doubted he shared her feelings.

"We may actually get along if we get hitched."

"How romantic." She slid from the bed and rummaged through her drawer for something to wear. She decided on a pair of shorts and red tank. As she dressed, she turned and narrowed her eyes at him. "The idea that we would stop fighting is absurd."

"Is it really?"

She couldn't answer. Confusion held her tongue. Her mind raced, yet she could not settle on a single word. His hurt look penetrated to her core. Someone knocked on the front door. The interruption shattered the tension.

"Who the hell is that?" Abe snapped. "The first time in my life I ask a woman to marry me, and although it wasn't the most romantic proposal, it's interrupted."

"Maybe it's Sheriff Stansey?"

He shook his head.

When he didn't get up, she sighed. "I'll get it. Though I know I must look like I've been through a hurricane." She patted her tangled hair.

"Do we have to?" he grumbled.

"Whoever it is knows we're here."

"Then let me get it."

Abe left the room while she quickly brushed her hair, wiped the messy mascara from beneath her eyes, and headed downstairs. She heard the faint sounds of conversation in the kitchen and found Abe sitting at the table with an attractive blonde.

The woman turned her bright blue gaze on Dee. Hoping this wasn't yet another woman Abe hadn't told her about, Dee prepared herself. This woman looked more like Abe's type. Elegant and gorgeous.

She stood. The woman's tall stature dwarfed Dee, making her sigh. Was she a model?

"You must be the newcomer I've heard so much about."

She nodded slowly. "Yes, I'm Dee."

"We've never had the pleasure of meeting." The woman extended a slender, finely manicured hand. "I'm Alexis Lauder, Matt's wife."

"Nice to meet you." A diamond sparkled on Alexis's ring finger, catching Dee's attention when she shook her hand. Unbidden, the memory of Matt's advances returned, making her squirm.

"My husband came to your party, but I was out of town visiting my parents," Alexis said.

"Yes, he told me. Florida, right?"

"Yes, in Clearwater. Abe asked me in. I hope that's okay." Alexis fidgeted with her gold chain necklace.

"More than okay." Dee shot a look at a brooding Abe. "Did your children have a good time visiting?"

Alexis's face lit up. "Yes, very much. They're enjoying the summer."

Abe rose from the chair and circled the table. Dee sucked in a deep breath as his hand pressed the small of her back.

"Did I interrupt something?" Alexis took a step toward the door.

"Yes," Abe said.

"No," Dee answered at the same time.

Alexis looked from one to the other. "Umm...I can come back later."

"We wouldn't hear of such a thing--right Abe?" Dee twisted around and glowered at him.

One corner of his mouth lifted. "Of course not. I was just proposing to Dee. No problem."

Alexis's mouth fell open. All color drained from her face. "I'm sorry." She started toward the door again.

Dee pulled herself together. "He's only joking." She attempted a laugh.

"Was I?" Abe said in her ear.

She turned to face him again. "Abe, you stop that. She'll think you're being serious."

A slow smile curved his mouth. His eyes twinkled. "I'm known for my sense of humor."

"Oh." Alexis shifted uncomfortably.

Dee felt her cheeks flush. Abe caught her with a pinch on the backside; she jumped and squealed.

"You sure are jittery this morning, Dee." Abe chuckled. "Don't drink too much coffee. I hear caffeine can make a person anxious."

She restrained a powerful urge to pinch him back. "Don't you have something to do, Abe, so Alexis and I can get to know each other better?"

"Yeah, I guess I do have a few things to do on the farm." He crossed the room toward the door. One hand on the screen, he stopped and caught Dee's eye. "We'll talk later."

Abe gone, Dee turned to Alexis. "Would you like a glass of lemonade?"

"Would love one."

Dee and Alexis walked outside and sat on the porch to enjoy the beautiful, clear morning. Alexis smiled. "You're one lucky gal, you know?"

"What do you mean?" Dee asked over the rim of her glass.

"Not only is Abe a hunk of a man, but he's got brains and brawn to boot," Alexis said.

Dee swallowed her lemonade in one gulp. "He can be a stubborn ass though."

"Can't they all?" Alexis laughed and threaded her fingers through her hair. "But don't you deny it, girl. Your secret, if it is a secret, is safe with me. I'm delighted by the idea."

Dee looked at the other woman. "Is it that obvious?"

Alexis nodded. "Like I said, you're fortunate." She sighed. "If Matt would look at me the way Abe looks at you, with such raw desire, I'd swing like a monkey from a tree." She fanned her face.

"I...I don't think he..."

"Oh, come on!" Alexis laughed. "A woman must know when a man is in love with her."

Although the conversation was deep for two people who'd only just met, Dee enjoyed talking with Alexis and believed they could be good friends. "I'm not sure if love is what Abe is feeling," Dee admitted with a frown.

Alexis blinked. "Well, Abe Delaney is off the market, and there'll be many ladies with broken hearts all over Willow Creek." She laughed. "Especially one in particular."

"Melissa?"

Alexis narrowed her almond-shaped eyes. Her round, pretty face hardened. "You bet. She'll have her claws in another man soon enough. Maybe this time he'll reciprocate the feelings."

"She seems like she just wants to be loved. Sometimes that can make a person do desperate things."

Alexis looked shocked. "You're very generous." Her voice turned icy and her eyes grew dark. "I wish I could be."

Dee's eyes widened. "I'm sensing a little hostility."

"You bet your best pair of stilettos it's hostility," Alexis replied bitterly. "Oh, my husband denied the affair, but the signs were unmistakable."

So, Mayor Matt Lauder was a womanizer. No surprise. "With Melissa?"

The other woman nodded curtly, then peered out over the tops of the trees. "I can't pin all the blame on Matt. Our marriage had never been perfect. In fact, not even civil most of the time. 'Romantic' has never been a word I could use to describe our relationship, but for some odd reason I agreed to marry him. He always seemed half with me and half somewhere else, or with someone else."

A lump caught in Dee's throat. The words were like an axe, cutting open the memory of her engagement to Jacob. "I'm sorry to hear that."

Alexis laughed. "Some people can be content with less than what I have. So, who am I to complain? My children are my world."

Dee kept quiet.

"Oh, my. Here I've meandered on about my problems, and forgotten what brought me out here. It's been a long time since I've had someone to talk to who'll just listen." She sighed. A smile came back over her delicate features. "Matt is planning a business party next week, and I need a caterer. I've heard you have a catering business."

"Well, I did--or at least my mother did. She and I partnered together," Dee said.

"Then it looks like I've struck gold."

Dee hesitated. "I'm not sure... Did you say it's next week?"

"It's only a small gathering, no more than ten people. Mostly the county commissioners, a couple of deep pockets, people that can help further Matt's career." Alexis crinkled her nose.

"Do you know what you're wanting? A buffet or a sit down dinner?"

Alexis looked baffled. Her red lips thinned. "No, I guess I haven't thought much about it."

"Why don't I take a few days and plan out some ideas, and you can choose?"

"Thanks, that would be great. I'm glad I came." Alexis lowered her eyes "I feel better."

"Feel better?" Dee questioned.

Alexis hesitated. "I needed to know if my husband had approached you yet, you know, to show you his worth in gold, if you know what I mean?"

Dee started to open her mouth, but Alexis added, "But after I see the heated passion between you and Abe, I feel secure that my charming husband doesn't stand a chance."

"Alexis, even if Abe and I weren't an item, I still wouldn't be interested in a married man."

Alexis's eyes misted. "I believe you. It's pathetic that I must investigate every pretty woman that wanders into town." She sighed. "But I'm glad I came."

Dee sat on the porch long after Alexis had gone. Why did Alexis stay in a seemingly unhappy marriage? As if she had a right to question Alexis's marriage when her relationship with Jacob had been just as cold. Dee wouldn't have stayed with Jacob long. She would have moved on.

Life was too short to live miserably. She wanted love and to be loved, above and beyond two people merely living together because it simply worked. She wanted a man who cared for her so deeply he couldn't imagine life without her.

Did Abe love her? Could he feel such deep emotion for her?

She wouldn't settle for any less. Not this time around.

Abe strolled up the yard toward the house. She watched him. Her breath caught as she admired his shirtless chest and six-pack abs. He looked delicious. Toned and perfect in every way.

His worn, low-rise jeans sat on his lean hips. The material stretched across his powerful legs. His hair was damp, probably from sweating, and she wanted nothing more than to rub all over his dewy body. With each step that brought him closer, his magnetism drew her deeper.

He approached the porch and shot her a glance. A mischievous smile spread over his face.

"Your eyes are cutting right through me." He draped his arms over the top railing.

The muscles in his arms bulged. She imagined them wrapped around her, holding her, connecting with her. "You're half-naked. I can't help myself."

"I like that look in your eyes," he said, his voice low.

She swept her tongue across her lips. "I wish I could lie. If I could, I'd tell you that you have no effect on me."

He reached across the short distance and played with the hem of her shirt. "Is that what you want, to have no feelings for me? What fun would that be?"

"And deny myself this dream? Never."

His eyes locked with hers. She got up from the rocker and stepped toward him, placing both hands on his shoulders. He dropped his head against her stomach and growled.

"I need to protect you. I'm restless and can't seem to relax. I feel like I'm wearing someone else's skin."

"So I'm not the only one in agony, huh?" she whispered.

He drew away, circled the porch railing as fast as his long, lean legs would carry him and made his way up the stairs and over to her. In one swift move, he swept her up into his arms and held her against his body. "I'd love to take you upstairs and make love to you until the moon rises."

"What about Sheriff Stansey?"

"I have a confession to make." He nuzzled her neck. "I called Stansey and told him to wait. The locksmith won't be here until the end of the week. I've got you all to myself...and I believe I asked you a question."

"You've gone to some trouble." She kissed his warm cheek.

"How do you feel about the part where I take you upstairs and make love to you?"

"Well, let's see..." She twirled a lock of his thick black hair playfully around her finger as he carried her through the front door. "That could be very dangerous."

"Dangerous?" he whispered in her ear.

"Did you have your extra protein this morning?"

"And a vitamin." He stopped at the stairs and kissed her urgently, searing her to the bone. His breathing grew hoarse as he carried her up the stairs and into his bedroom and laid her on the bed.

She reached for him, but he moved away. Stripping out of his jeans and boxers, he lay next to her.

"Abe?" she whispered.

"Hmm?"

"Is lust enough to keep two people together?"

He pulled back. "Is that what we have, lust?"

His look speared into her. She smiled and wrapped her arms around his neck and pulled him closer. "Whatever it is it feels pretty close to heaven, doesn't it?"

"I want you to be mine." He feathered kisses along her jaw line.

"Please..." She laid her head back into the pillow. He took the opportunity to kiss her neck.

He drew her closer against his naked body, as gently as if she were made of delicate glass. He undressed her slowly and languidly. Moments ticked by in bliss. His fingers swept across her skin, sending shivers of anticipation through her. He bent his mouth and kissed her flesh along her hip bone. She arched as he stroked her. He finally brought his lips back to hers. His kiss left her floating, until she clung to him as if he could anchor her to earth.

His hand slid down her neck, over her warm skin, to her sensitive breasts, grazing them with rough palms. A moan escaped her lips as she buried her fingers through his hair. When his hand slid between her legs, she trembled.

She called out his name and slid her hands down his back. He cupped her buttocks, bringing her off the bed. "I want all of you, Dee."

Didn't he already know she was his, and had been for a long time? She couldn't imagine another man sparking such intense emotion and desire within her.

She melted like butter under his touch, incapable of doing anything but capturing every touch, every feeling, and every beat of his heart. Fire turned to ice, bursting into shards of ecstasy that left them each glowing like embers of golden light.

Sated and basking in Abe's warmth, Dee drifted into sleep.

When she awoke, the setting sun shadowed the room. She stretched like a lazy cat and reached for Abe's warm body, but came up depressingly empty-handed. She rose out of bed. Where was he?

She pulled on a tee from his drawer and descended the stairs barefoot. She found him before the stove in the kitchen, dressed in only a pair of white boxers. He looked devilishly handsome. "The bed was cold without you," she said.

"Sorry. I needed nourishment." He reached for two plates and filled each with slices of ham, scrambled eggs, and buttered toast. "I had hoped to serve you in bed."

"I'm starving."

"Sit and eat." He placed a plate for her at the table.

"This looks yummy." Forking up the eggs, she noticed her purse sitting on the table. She smiled. "Did Sheriff Stansey stop by?" The purse was dirty and shabby, but as she rummaged inside she found everything where it belonged.

Except the house keys.

"He did. He didn't like it when I told him he wasn't going to disturb you, but he gave in and left with one condition. You gotta go down to the station first thing tomorrow morning and make a statement."

"I must have been sleeping like a baby not to hear him knock."

"You definitely didn't look like a baby."

"Oh really?"

He grinned. "You looked like a wanton woman. Your hair was spread over the pillow and the blanket had fallen away. You made your man very happy last night."

Her heart sped up. *Her man.* She liked that. She dug into the eggs.

"Dee." Something in his voice stopped her with her fork halfway to her lips. "If lust was the only feeling between us, I wouldn't have asked you to marry me."

She dropped her fork back to the plate. "Then why, Abe?"

"Because marriage is right for us."

"There's more to marriage than being right, Abe. Whatever 'right' means." Her stomach churned. "We could fight like cats and dogs and end up hating one another."

"I've thought about that." He picked up his fork and began shoving egg into his mouth. He swallowed a sip of coffee before adding, "You're hard-headed and stubborn as hell most of the time, at least when it comes to our relationship."

She tensed, eyeing him. "Have you reflected on your own stellar qualities?"

"Just this morning, in fact." He winked.

She pushed her chair back and fled the kitchen. She raced up the stairs, Abe close on her heels.

"Dee!"

"Can't we just live in the moment?" She crested the top step and spun to glare at him. "Can't we stop arguing for once?"

Before he could respond, she retreated to his bedroom and fell onto the messy bed, burying her face in her hands.

"Dee?" He knelt at the bedside. "Is marrying me a betrayal to Jacob?"

"No."

"I'm still on the fence," he admitted. "Every time I kiss you, in the back of my mind I think I'm somehow betraying my brother."

Guilt darkened his eyes and creased his mouth. She couldn't take it anymore. She had to tell him the truth. "Abe, there's something I have to tell you."

She wanted to blurt it out, empty her heart and soul, but made herself hold back and choose her words carefully.

"My relationship with Jacob wasn't what it had seemed--or maybe it was exactly what it seemed. Either way, it was just a facade."

"Facade?"

"To say the least." She clasped her hands tightly in her lap. "When I met your brother, I thought he was handsome, sweet and funny. He could always make me laugh." She smiled. "Our relationship was whirlwind, from the time we met until I agreed to marry him not much later. I thought I would be all right learning about him as time passed."

"That was Jacob, rushing through things headlong." Abe smiled.

"It wasn't until our first night here that I realized things weren't as perfect as I'd believed. Something just wasn't right." She lowered her eyes. The memory that left a bad taste in her mouth. "He assured me that it wasn't me, but it was still a blow to my ego." She looked up, only to watch doubt flicker through Abe's eyes. "I couldn't help but think there was something wrong with me because he couldn't make love to me."

* * * *

Abe got up and moved away from her. He needed space, and leaned against the dresser. Was what she was saying true? They hadn't consummated their relationship? Despite all of his questions, he kept quiet, allowing her to finish.

"We were happy, at least to a point, until we came here. That's when everything began to take a turn for the worse. I couldn't understand what was so wrong with me that my fiancé didn't want to have sex with me. I knew he wasn't out to hurt me, so how could I be angry with him? Then when he told me the truth, it all made sense."

"The truth?" Abe probed.

"Your brother was in love with someone else."

Abe swept a hand through his hair. He returned to the bedside, but didn't sit down. "Then why the hell did he ask you to marry him?" If his brother were still alive, Abe would have throttled him.

"I asked the same question. He wanted a wife and children. He wanted everyone around him happy. I even understood why he felt such turmoil, trying to please everyone, instead of just pleasing himself. He realized that once we were married he couldn't lie. That's why I'd promised to keep his secret safe and not leave him right away. He wanted to tell people the truth when the time was right."

"Secret?"

She nodded. "Jacob had no attraction for me."

Abe narrowed his eyes. "Was he completely insane? Must have been to not find you attractive."

She shook her head. "The person he loved wasn't at the same point Jacob was. They'd split up. Jacob thought he could move on, but he realized once he brought me here he couldn't follow through with the marriage." She pinched the bridge of her nose.

"Who is she--the person he was in love with?"

"I don't know. He wouldn't tell. He promised to keep their relationship a secret. He only told me what he wanted me to know, which wasn't a lot. They were having a secret affair. The secret wasn't Jacob's sexuality. Jacob wanted to be who he was without the constraints of secrecy. The man he was in a relationship with didn't see it the same way. He made Jacob feel guilty, like they should be ashamed, of their relationship. Jacob knew he had no reason to feel shame because he was gay."

A harsh bark of laughter escaped before he could stop it. "I thought I heard you say he was gay."

Her eyes were dark, her mouth unsmiling. "That's what I said. I wouldn't joke about something like that."

All of the missing pieces came together into a single puzzle. Jacob's secretive and ever-changing behavior. His frequent long trips. His whispered phone calls. "Why didn't he tell me?" Abe mumbled.

"He wanted to tell you. I think he was afraid you'd find out who he was seeing. It was a long-term relationship, one Jacob held dear to his heart, but he was bound by his partner's need for privacy."

"Privacy? How could I have not known?" His heart skipped a beat. "I loved my brother, no matter what. Did I somehow make him believe that I wouldn't understand? I could have respected the need for privacy. Hell, I would have clobbered anyone who dared say anything." He paced the room. "But what about you, Dee? Where did you fit into all of this?"

"He tried." She cleared her throat. "There was a connection between us. We cared for each other, like a brother and sister would. He thought that was enough, and I believe he truly meant for us to be married, have kids, live happily. Jacob was fond of the idea of having kids, being a father. But just like anyone who has loved and lost, the tenderness remains in their heart, no matter how we wish it would disappear. Jacob couldn't move on. He always found himself going back."

"You have no idea who he was seeing? This man who kept my brother chained in lies?"

She shrugged. "I don't know. I'm not sure he ever would have told me."

"You accepted his affair. It had nothing to do with his sexuality, but everything to do with trust. He was unfaithful to you."

"Yes." She tugged her hair away from her face. "But in some people's eyes I was equally unfaithful."

"How?"

"By the time he had told me the truth, I had gone completely numb to him and the idea of marriage. I cared for him, but not like one would a husband. I felt released, and relieved of my obligations and responsibilities. I had moved on. I had given my heart away to the man who still owns it."

"Yet you couldn't trust me enough to tell me the truth a long time ago." He couldn't even look at her. He leaned against the dresser. "I don't know if I should be angrier with you or Jacob for not telling me what I deserved to know."

"I don't blame you for being upset. I understand this is a lot to learn." She nodded. "I promised I wouldn't divulge his secret, Abe. You must understand the loyalty."

"He's dead, Dee. That negates the promise, don't you think?"

She shook her head. Her hair bounced around her shoulders. "How should I know, Abe? This is something I've had weighing my shoulders from the day he told me."

Abe sucked in a painful breath. "I need to take a walk."

"Okay."

Abe stalked from the room, raced down the stairs and rushed out the front door. Disappointment surged through his veins. All those years of suffering...useless, wasted.

He headed across the grass toward the barn, clenching his hands into fists. The breeze did nothing to cool his heated fury. He craved a smoke, but refused. Apparently he'd picked the wrong time to quit.

He didn't like feeling betrayed. Or stupid.

How could he have missed the truth for so many years? The proof had been right in front of his eyes the entire time. Yet he'd never suspected Jacob hid a secret he would take to his grave.

Chapter 17

Dee crawled out of her bed and forced the burning nausea back down her throat. Her head tingled with the onset of a terrible headache. She blamed it on stress. She'd been on a roller coaster since she'd arrived in Willow Creek.

After she dressed and brushed her teeth, she still felt sick. A rough, restless night hadn't helped. After Abe had stormed out of the house, she'd returned to her own room. She'd hoped he would come to her after he settled down, but as stubborn as Abe was, she guessed he needed a little longer to cool off.

He had every right to be confused. When Jacob had told her, she'd been floored.

She went downstairs to the kitchen. Maybe some toast would calm her rumbling intestines. Yet Dee nearly jumped out of her socks when she saw who sat at the table. "Mitch, what are you doing here?"

He got up, looking her over from head to toe. "You should know a cowboy always comes home." He gave her hand a friendly squeeze. "You sure are a sight for sore eyes."

"But I thought you were trying to patch things up with your wife." she said. Unhappiness swept across his face. Dee winced. "I'm sorry. It didn't work, did it?"

"I called Abe. He said I could come back."

She heard a rustling in the pantry and turned as Abe walked out. He looked up. Their eyes met. Hurt flashed through his eyes. His disheveled hair, shadowed chin and the dark circles under his eyes told her he hadn't slept well either. Abe poured creamer into his cup. The chill of his presence touched her from across the room, raising her hackles.

She offered Mitch a forced smile. "Well, I'm glad you're back, though I wish things had worked out."

"I'm glad, too."

She kept her eyes on Abe's back. "Mitch, can I talk to Abe alone?"

Mitch didn't say a word. She heard his footsteps, then the door clicked shut behind him. She sighed. "You can't block me out, Abe. We've shared way too much."

"I'm not blocking you out." Abe's face pinched.

"Okay then, running from the issue." She shook her head.

"I'm here. Let's discuss it."

"I'd like that." She wanted to cry. When had she become such an emotional wreck?

"Dee, I'm not pushing you away. I needed space."

She leaned against the counter. "Very interesting. You ask me to marry you one minute, and the next tell me you need space. An engaged couple must learn to communicate."

"An engaged couple? You haven't even agreed to my proposal."

She kept her eyes off him and on her toast. "Apparently your proposal wasn't even genuine."

"How do you get that?"

She went to the refrigerator, grabbed the butter and snagged a knife from the drawer. "I can't marry a man who can't share his feelings."

"You should reflect on your own actions. You held a secret about your relationship with *my* brother for years."

She dropped the knife. It struck the counter with a loud *ding.* "Okay, fair's fair, but Jacob's secret wasn't mine to tell."

"That's bullshit." He rubbed the back of his neck. "You didn't tell me out of spite."

She planted her fists on her hips. Anger pulsated through her veins. "I didn't tell you because he was gone. It didn't really matter anymore."

He opened his mouth, then slammed it shut. "Then why did you tell me now?"

"Because I couldn't stand another second of your guilt." She picked the knife back up.

"I feel as small as an ant right now. I think you want to castrate me." He eyes fell to the knife then back on her. "I can't think." One corner of his mouth lifted.

"I can't help it." She couldn't hold back the tears any longer.

"Oh hell, Dee." He bent close and drew her gaze into his.

She began to cry even harder, and swiped at the wetness with her sleeve. "You should go. Maybe we both need some time away from each other."

"How did I know this would turn around and make me out to be the bad guy?"

She sighed. "You're not the bad guy. No one is." She tossed the knife into the sink and sniffled. "I don't understand what's wrong with me." Her words fell from the tail end of a sob.

"You look pale. Are you okay?"

She nodded. "I'll be fine." She tried to control her tears and failed. "Are you still angry?"

He brushed her hair away from her face, where it stuck to her wet cheek. "I'm not angry with you. I regret that things weren't handled differently. I had a long time to think things through, and you did what you thought was best. It's too bad you had to carry Jacob's secret all this time. I guess I didn't make it easy for Jacob to tell me, but I can't go back."

"Neither of us can."

He pulled her against his chest, and she melted. "Better now?"

"Uh-huh." She didn't want to move.

"I've gotta make a trip into town later and run some errands. Will you be okay with Mitch?"

She rubbed her nose. "Yes."

"You won't run away again, will you?"

"I'll be here." She stepped upon tiptoes and kissed him lightly on the cheek. "As long as I know we're past last night's revelation, and can head into a future."

"It's not easy realizing I've been an ass on more than one occasion. I've lost a lot of precious time."

"I should have told you the truth long ago, but I promised Jacob."

"I should have known." He shook his head. "I might not be back until late this evening."

"You're being vague."

"Not on purpose."

She rolled her eyes but let it go. "I'll be busy anyway."

"Really?"

"I didn't get a chance to tell you." Moving to the other side of the counter, she poured herself a cup of coffee and nibbled her toast. He watched her with narrowed eyes.

"Are you going to tell me now?"

"Of course." She wrinkled her nose. "Alexis has asked me to cater a small business dinner for her husband. Might help drum up business, if I decide to buy that diner in town."

"Buy the diner?" His eyes widened.

"Is there a problem with that?"

He leaned against the counter. "Not at all. In fact, I think it's a great idea." He tapped the tip of her nose. "And it means you'll be staying." He smiled.

She slid her hand up his chest. "Interesting how things can change. It feels like only yesterday, you wanted nothing more than to see me packing."

"Sometimes a man needs to admit he's wrong. But fair warning, don't get your hopes up about the Lauder party. Alexis generally tolerates the man for a short while, then leaves town again. In fact, I thought Matt was living with his parents."

"Did Melissa tell you this?" When he nodded, she sighed. "That shouldn't surprise me."

He stared at her. "What do you mean?"

"Alexis told me Matt had an affair with Melissa. I don't know when it began or ended, but it was an affair." She popped a piece of toast in her mouth.

He laughed. "Melissa and Matt? Never."

"How can you be sure?"

"Because." He grabbed a piece of her toast and bit into it. "She despises Matt. That's the kindest way to put it. She thinks he's odd."

"That makes two of us." She started to tell him about what had happened at the hardware store, but decided against it. "He seems...hmm, can't quite think of the right word."

"He wasn't like that back in high school. In fact, I don't remember him changing until after graduation. But then, don't we all change after we get out of school?"

"He talked to me at the party and it was very uncomfortable," she added. "Later, I caught him staring at me."

"Honey, there were lots of men--and women--staring at you that night. You know we don't get many newcomers in these parts. Anyway, I think Matt wants everyone to believe he's a ladies' man."

"Alexis is gorgeous, sexy to boot. If he cheated, I just don't understand why."

He tilted his head and studied her. "A lot of men cheat, pretty wife or not." Jacob's memory hung between them like a silent specter. Abe's chocolate gaze caressed her. He took her shoulders into his hands. "But I never will."

A wave of dizziness made the room spin. She grabbed his arm for support. She blinked. "I think I'm coming down with a bug. But I can't get sick. I've lots of planning to do for the Lauder party, if it doesn't fall through."

"You give M.J. one helluva party, you hear? Maybe it'll help with his and Alexis's marriage."

"M.J.?"

"M.J. is Matt's nickname. His real name is Matthew Jason. He didn't become Matt until he came back from college. I guess he just grew out of the old nickname."

"M.J." She fiddled with the name. "Why does that name sound familiar?"

"Maybe because Jacob mentioned the name in passing. They were pretty good friends during school. They hung out a lot because they played football and basketball, and had the same friends."

"Maybe." She sighed.

"I don't want to talk about the Lauders anymore. Go riding with me, Dee." Her mouth fell open. "Close your mouth, sweetheart, before you let a fly in." He laughed as she snapped her mouth closed. "You heard me right. Come riding with me before I leave."

"Uhh--"

"You trust me, don't you?"

"Of course." There was no one she trusted more.

"Then trust me enough to keep you safe. We'll ride double. You haven't seen the property since you've been back. It's beautiful with the new trees and the groves."

She looked into his eyes. All fear vanished as a feeling of security took its place. "Okay."

"I think it's time we both laid our guilt and fear to rest. I've punished myself enough over the years by allowing guilt to keep me from the things I love."

She swallowed. Was he talking about more than just riding?

"Meet me by the stables in twenty," he said.

When Dee rounded the barn she found Abe waiting by the stables, leaning against the wooden fence with one leg propped up on the rail. One of the stable hands had just finished tightening Sally's girth strap, and now stepped back to let Abe swing up into the saddle. He looked regal and comfortable atop the horse. Pride swelled in Dee's chest as she took in his smile. She guessed he'd expected her to back out, but it was time she overcame her fear.

He held out his hand. "Ready?"

"Ready as I'll ever be." Terror slithered its way along her spine and constricted her throat, but there was no hesitation when she placed her palm into his. He lifted her with ease and she settled into the saddle behind him. She leaned into his back and wrapped her arms around his waist, breathing in the masculine scent of him. Pressing her ear close, she listened to the faint beat of his heart. The rhythmic thumping and his warmth calmed her.

He ran his hand down Sally's neck and patted her firmly. "Let's go, girl." With a gentle tug of the reins, Sally moved slowly away from the fence.

The ache in Dee's arms made her realize just how hard she was gripping Abe's waist. She loosened her hold as her muscles relaxed enough for her to sit up and look around. She enjoyed the beauty of the land. There was a sense of freedom, with the wind flowing through her hair and the power of the horse underneath her. She felt a little guilty that Abe kept Sally at a slow trot, likely for her benefit. She wasn't quite ready for a thunderous gallop, but maybe in time she'd be as comfortable in the saddle as Abe.

They reached the blueberry grove and Abe climbed down. She threw her leg over the side and looked at the ground. "You made that look easy."

He laughed. "Let me help." He wrapped his hands around her waist and lifted her to the ground. Yet when her feet touched the earth, he didn't let her go. He held her close, burying his nose in her hair and nuzzling her neck.

"Mm." She turned her head to give him better access. "Did you bring me all the way out here to see the land, or did you have something else in mind?"

"That almost sounds like an offer, sweetheart." His voice was husky.

She reached her arms around his neck and stood on tiptoes. "Thank you," she said.

"For?"

"For being my strength and encouraging me when I need it."

He slipped his hand around and cradled the back of her neck as he dropped his lips to hers. The kiss was full of passion and need. "I'd like to take this further--" His words were close to a growl. "--but we're not alone."

She pulled back. "Huh?"

He gave a jerky head nod. "Company." She followed his gaze. Coming up over the hill was a ranch truck.

As it pulled up, she saw the driver: Mitch. He climbed out and looked from Abe to Dee, then back to Abe apologetically. "Didn't mean to interrupt, but the vet is here and wants to speak to you about the new horse. Looks like he has colic."

Abe shook his head and looked at her with a frown. "I need to take care of this."

She nodded. "Of course."

"You mind riding back with Mitch?"

"Go on, Abe. I'll be fine." He gave her a quick peck on the lips, then moved toward Sally and lifted himself in the saddle. With a click of his tongue and a nudge of his boot, Sally took off, hooves pounding the dirt and mane blowing.

"I didn't know you were up here with him. Sorry I barged in," Mitch said.

"It's okay." She turned and smiled. "I have to run into town anyway."

After she slid into the passenger seat and Mitch took the wheel, he said, "I'll take you into town."

She eyed his profile. "Did Abe ask you to baby sit me?"

He shook his head. "No."

"He didn't?"

He didn't take his eyes off the trail as they headed toward the house. "He asked me to watch over you."

Dee sighed. She understood Abe's concern, but she didn't want or need a babysitter. "I'll be fine. I'll be at Alexis Lauder's, and I'll be back. Then, I promise you can hang out with me and play bodyguard. Deal?"

He laughed and shrugged. "Deal."

They hit a pothole. Dee grabbed the safety bar and braced herself. "The ride on Sally was much smoother."

"You just might turn out to be a farm girl after all."

"Just maybe." For the first time, she felt like she belonged. The look she'd seen in Abe's eyes before Mitch pulled up had told her everything she needed to know.

Abe needed her, too.

Her heart swelled. Life was coming full circle. And somehow she felt like she owed Jacob. Even through the pain he'd caused, without him she'd have never found Abe. She'd only wished he would have found his own happiness in life.

She wondered who the man was who'd stripped Jacob of his happiness. Who had he loved so deeply that it had been more a cage than freedom? She made a mental inventory of all the townspeople, but came up blank.

They pulled up to the house, and she pushed the thought away. The answer was buried with Jacob.

* * * *

An hour later, Dee pulled up in front of the Lauder house and parked on the street. The house was a lovely Victorian, painted pale yellow with green shutters.

Alexis opened the door, stunning in a silk shirt and tan slacks. "Matt's mother just picked up the kids and took them to the park." She enveloped Dee in a tight hug. "Come to the kitchen. I've got a pot full of tea waiting." She led the way into the large, modern kitchen.

"Is Matt home?" Dee asked.

Alexis sighed. "No, he had business to attend to...again." She waved it off.

As Alexis poured tea into a porcelain cup, her hand shook. The tea spilled all over the granite countertop. "Oh, great. I'm such a klutz."

"Here, let me help with that." Dee used her napkin to wipe it up. "Are you okay?"

"I've decided to leave Matt for good." The words tumbled out.

"You have?"

She nodded. "Our marriage has been over for years. I just refused to believe it. I thought after the affair with Melissa ended, things would change, and he would make an effort. He did for a while, but it didn't last." She swept back her bangs.

"Have you told him?"

Alexis nodded. "Almost an hour ago. He flipped out. He screamed and called me names." Her hands twisted together. "He wasn't himself, Dee. He made threats."

"Threats?"

Alexis sighed. "He didn't make any sense. He said he would make people pay for screwing his life. The time had come for vindication. He just...lost it. He's been behaving oddly, and I think he's dangerous. I told him not to come back here until the kids and I are gone."

Dee sat forward on the seat and asked gently. "Alexis, I know this is a difficult time for you, but are you certain he had an affair with Melissa?"

She shifted her blue gaze from Dee to the table. "I found a letter addressed to him signed by her. She asked, or more demanded, that he meet her because they weren't through." Alexis took a long ragged breath. "I had suspected he was having an affair, with all of the late night phone calls and trips away from town."

"Did you confront Melissa?" Dee asked.

"I really don't think--" Alexis stopped.

"I'm sorry. I shouldn't pry."

Alexis reached over and touched Dee's arm. "I meant I really didn't know what to do. I was embarrassed, shamed and depressed. Not only was he my husband, but she was my friend, a good friend."

"Do you think the letter may have meant something other than the obvious?" Dee asked. Abe had insisted Melissa and Matt weren't having an affair. She believed him. So who was Matt sleeping with?

"How many years ago was this?"

"It's been a long time. Seven years, but there have been others since." Alexis looked at Dee strangely. "Has Melissa said something to you?"

"No, I promise," Dee said. "I guess I just feel connected to you. While I was engaged to Jacob, he had an affair, too," she admitted.

Alexis sighed and sniffled. "I didn't know him well, but he was very good friends with Matt."

"I thought that was only in school? I mean, I didn't remember them hanging out too much."

Alexis seemed almost baffled at that. "They hung out all of the time. They went away on fishing trips every summer. Matt even accompanied Jacob to out-of-town horse shows."

"Fishing? Jacob hated fishing." Dee laughed, then stilled, her breath catching. Oh...oh no...

"Are you okay, Dee?" Alexis frowned.

Dee stood. A bout of dizziness washed over her. She clung to the chair until she regained her equilibrium "Has Matt gone fishing lately?" she asked.

Alexis thought a moment before shrugging. "Actually, since you mention, it no. Not since Jacob's accident."

"I've got to go, Alexis." Dee headed for the door.

Alexis followed. "Dee what's wrong? Please, tell me."

Dee turned to a bewildered Alexis and said, "It wasn't Melissa."

"What? How do you know that?"

"Ask your husband."

Dee climbed into her Jeep and slammed on the gas. Her wheels squealed loudly as she pulled away from the street. She knew exactly who Matt held responsible in his psychotic delusion: her. And if Alexis called and told him about her and Dee's discussion, he'd be out for blood. She believed Alexis. Matt was dangerous. Knowing he'd lost his wife and children would only push him over the edge further, if not completely.

She fumbled for the cellphone buried in her purse, spilling the contents in her haste. Her mind raced. It took a long moment before she finally punched in the correct number. Each time voice mail answered, Dee hung up and called back. On the fourth attempt, Melissa finally answered.

"It's Dee--"

"Hell's bells, woman. I'm in the middle of giving a perm."

"I'm going to ask you a very odd question, and it's important that you answer in all honesty."

There was a long pause before Melissa finally answered, "O-kaaay."

"Did you have an affair with Matt Lauder?"

Her laughter rang over the line. "Are you kidding me?" Melissa snorted. "I hate that man, and he knows it. I'd have to be blind, insane, and desperate to do that. No, on second thought, I'd still turn the rat down."

"Then why did you send him a letter insinuating that there was some sort-of business between the two of you?"

Everything went eerily silent. Dee didn't think she would get a response until, Melissa said softly, "I don't know how you know about that letter, and I'm not sure I want to talk about this."

"Melissa, tell me. I wouldn't ask if it wasn't important." She pressed her temples. "I know I'm asking you some personal questions, but I need to know, please."

"It wasn't a love letter," Melissa said.

Dee sighed. "I'm sorry, Melissa, someone is calling, and my phone is beeping. Did you say it wasn't a love letter?"

"Not in any way, shape or form, trust me."

"Then you knew he was having an affair, right?"

"Dee, I caught him cheating. I told him he had two options. Either he could tell Alexis the truth or I would. The lousy bastard must have lied and told her he slept with me. People have a way of believing the worst about me, just because I'm not married. He's not my type. Size does matter." The bitterness was evident.

"You're wrong--"

"Honey, size does matter."

"I'm not talking about that. I don't care about those details. I'm not sure Matt told Alexis who he slept with, but she assumed it was you because of the letter."

"What?" Melissa asked. "You broke up."

"I'll explain that later." She almost dropped the phone as she turned a sharp corner. "Who was he having an affair with, Melissa?"

There was a long, awkward silence before she finally answered. "I don't know. I was in Franklin buying supplies for the beauty shop. The warehouse is directly across from a seedy motel, popular for renting out rooms by the hour." She chuckled. "With all his family money, he couldn't pay a little extra for a room over at the Holiday Inn. There sat his fancy schmancy cherry red Porsche, smack dab in the parking lot without a care in the world that anyone, including his wife, could come along and see it there. That's Matt for you. His ego is bigger than Mount Fuji."

"But the letter, Melissa." Dee's phone beeped again as someone tried to get through. She ignored it. Her hand trembled and she barely kept the phone from shaking.

"I waited until he came out of the room, and watched him get into his car and pull away. I wanted to go and see the slut he'd been screwing. So I went to the door and knocked, but didn't get an answer." She clicked her tongue. "Let me just say that I'm not a snoop, but I had a feeling he was cheating with someone from around here and they were sneaking off to another town. I was desperate with curiosity."

"Who Melissa? Who was it?" Dee prompted.

"Hang on to your socks." Melissa hesitated. "I glanced inside the window and just about flipped when I saw a pair of men's cowboy boots and one of those silver horse buckles--you know, those one-of-a-kind ones on a black leather belt, sitting on the bed."

Dee's heart fell into her stomach. She knew exactly the kind of belt buckle she referred to. "Then you wrote the letter?"

"Not quite yet. I approached Matt and told him I knew about his little sideshow. I warned him Alexis wouldn't be happy to share him with another woman, or a man, for that matter. I didn't care who he was sleeping with. I only cared that he was screwing over my best friend. He was livid. Can you believe the bastard blew me off? I sent him the letter as a final warning. I felt sorry for Alexis because she was crazy in love with him. Matt was a good guy once upon a time, but something changed. I think the ladder to success clogged his brain."

"And Matt let Alexis find the letter," Dee murmured.

"And apparently Alexis believed what she wanted to believe. Busted, Matt allowed her to believe he slept with me instead of telling her the truth. He knew she'd never talk to me again after that. It's been years now, and she won't even look my way. She goes all the way to Franklin to get her hair done."

"He didn't want her to know that he was actually having an affair with..."

"Do you know who it was?" Melissa's voice rose in pitch.

"Do you know what day it was that you saw him at the motel?" Dee's stomach twisted into knots.

"Absolutely. The Fourth of July. I remember because I always go to the warehouse on that day, since my shop is closed for the holiday. They have a huge holiday sale and I can get my perm supplies for dirt--"

"I've gotta run." Dee turned the phone off. When she put it down, it slid off the seat onto the floorboard under her feet. She gave it a push with her toe, but didn't attempt to reach for it. It rang several times. She couldn't pull over. She needed to get back to the farm. Everything was falling together...or apart.

Dee parked in front of the house and dashed for the front door. "Mitch, are you here?" She needed someone to talk to. She needed help putting the puzzle together. Instinct told her there was an important piece missing.

Rather than wait for a response, she locked the door behind her, threw her keys on the table and headed down the basement stairs. She just knew she'd seen a box of Jacob's things in the basement and hoped his appointment book was in that box.

The box was exactly where she remembered it. She pushed away the cobwebs, grabbed the box and sat down on the floor with it. When she opened the lid, a waft of mildew violated her nostrils. Her stomach churned. Catching her breath, she flipped through the contents.

On his birthday, Dee had bought Jacob an expensive leather appointment book and planner and he had made a comment that he needed to keep better track of his comings and goings. Dee remembered being concerned that he seemed unusually distracted that evening. He'd told her he was fine, but had a friend who was having a difficult time. She hoped maybe something in the book could help her understand Jacob's life better. The last days of his life Jacob had seemed preoccupied, worried. Why?

The book was at the bottom of the box, its cover worn, stained with mildew. Cradling it as if it might break, she wiped off the dust. Open it, she told herself. Open it. The edges of half the pages were worn from handling, the rest even and smooth. She knew exactly where it stopped. August. The day Jacob had died, on his way back from some appointment no doubt written in this very book.

She swallowed the tightness in her throat, holding the book against her chest as if it could seal in her beating heart. She couldn't bring herself to look. Looking might raise questions she didn't want to ask, might force her to find answers she didn't want to know. His secrets were his. His world was his own. She hadn't belonged in it, hadn't wanted to know.

But it was time the secrets ended.

It was time she moved on.

She opened the cover. It crackled in protest. She skimmed date after date. Here and there were random notes about meeting M.J.

She flipped pages faster, plunging through April, May, June, July. *M.J., Shaker's. M.J., Park and Main, 9 PM.* She stopped on July. *M.J. Motel.* The evidence screamed at her in Jacob's handwriting. He'd been absent almost all of July. Business, he'd told her. Away on business. Business that involved meeting Matt in Franklin, apparently. She wondered how often.

Jacob's handwriting led her into August, like a looping path of black ink leading her further and further into the past. She stopped on the last page, heart roaring in violent beats. Coffee stained the paper, as if he'd dashed the note off in a hurry over breakfast. She'd gotten up early to make him cinnamon rolls that day, she remembered. He'd been scribbling in his planner, smiling to himself as he sipped his coffee. She'd wondered at the smile, small and almost secretive. Now she knew.

"He was with M.J. that day," she whispered. The words clogged in her closing throat; her eyes burned, vision blurring. "The day he died."

As she closed her eyes, the book fell from her fingers. It took a long moment before she felt in control. She opened her eyes, breathed in and exhaled.

Standing, she dusted herself off and went back upstairs. Abe would be home soon, and she planned to tell him everything. They could figure out together what to do.

She heard a key in the front door. The door creaked open, then banged closed. Footsteps trailed into the kitchen. It wasn't Abe. She knew Abe's firm, authoritative stride, stronger than this heavy clop. Must be Mitch. She slipped into the kitchen. "You'll never believe the day I've had--"

She stopped cold. So did he, smirking. Matt Lauder stood in the center of her kitchen, not five feet away.

Shit.

Dee held breathlessly still.

Matt looked like hell, as if someone had drained the life of him. He stared at her, eerily still, not a single muscle moving, not one eyelash twitching. His hair stood up everywhere; his red-rimmed eyes gleamed dark. His watchfulness, waiting and wary, reminded her of a rabid dog. A rabid dog in a suit, his tie crooked, a small rip in his left sleeve. A dark spot stained the lapel of his white shirt. Blood?

Her heart lurched. "What are you doing here?" He remained quiet. Her pulse quickened. "Are you okay, Matt?" she tried. "Can I get you a glass of water?" As she moved toward the sink, he took a step closer. She stopped.

"Let's cut the shit, shall we?" he said, harsh and low.

She lifted her chin. "I'm not sure what you mean."

He banged his fist onto the table. She jerked. The glass salt and pepper shakers bounced, then rolled onto the floor. "I don't like to play games, you bitch!" Anger radiated from him. Resentment and frustration twisted the pretty-boy face into a furious mask. "You and Alexis have a nice chat? Did she tell you she's leaving and taking my kids?"

One look in those burning eyes said he'd lost his grip, and would do anything to keep his secret. Would he believe her if she lied? Probably not, and she was tired of lies. "You're M.J."

One corner of his mouth twitched. "How did you figure it out? No one calls me that, not since I left for college." He took a step closer, menacing, but stopped when she retreated.

"Jacob had it written down in his appointment book." This was the man Jacob had loved? He was a creep, one whose very presence left her sick to her stomach. "Alexis doesn't know, does she?"

He clicked his tongue. "Everything was fine until you came back. Now I'll have to cover my tracks."

"Why not just tell Alexis the truth? It's who you are."

He stared at her, then barked a brittle laugh. "Do you think I've worked this hard building my career just to destroy it with a scandal? This isn't a place where people can be who they are. Alexis would have a field day running me through the cleaners. That's not happening. And she's not taking my kids."

"How do you plan to stop it?" Maybe if she kept him talking, she could reason with him.

"I didn't want it to come to this, Dee." He ignored her question. "I really didn't. Jacob cared for you. I believe he even loved you. He thought he could leave the past in the past and move on, have a couple of kids." His laugh was laced with bitterness. "I tried to warn you to leave town. Why couldn't you have listened?"

"You were the one who threw the brick through my window?" In the back of her mind, she'd known. She'd known before she'd even left his house. The hard evidence only brought the cold reality of it home, chilling her deep in her gut. This man had a problem--and he was very capable of causing her harm.

"It was only a brick. It wasn't like I hurt you." He shrugged. "And locking you in the basement was entertainment at its best. You used the damsel in distress routine and poor Abe fell for it. You two fucked that night. I bet he's a real tiger in bed."

She cringed. He'd been watching her with Abe. He took another ominous step toward her. She moved back until she pressed against the wall. She was trapped "You better leave, Matt. Mitch will be back any second now." Her voice cracked.

"Dee, do you think I'm stupid?"

Her heart sank. What had he done? "Is that Mitch's blood on your shirt?"

He looked down and scratched the spot with his nail. When he looked back at her, his face was devoid of emotion. "He won't be coming to your rescue, if that's what you'd hoped."

"If something happens to me, they'll know it was you."

"Why should I worry? Accidents happen." His eyes glittered with pride and malice. "I'm very good at making accidents happen."

Dee edged along the wall, a step closer to the door "Are you saying--" Her throat tightened until she couldn't breathe. "You killed Jacob?"

"It took you long enough, you idiot. Really, you should be thanking me. You had the hots for the older, tougher brother from the start. And Abe? Real swell guy, betraying his brother to get a piece of you." Matt's face sagged in a grotesque pantomime of grief. "Poor Jakey-boy. He knew you were screwing Abe, but he still loved you both. He was a fool. A sentimental fool who wanted his fiancée to love his brother just to ease his own guilt for not being what you deserved."

"Why kill Jacob?" Her legs quivered, threatening to dump her on the floor. She almost gave in, but that would leave him looming over her, at a distinct physical advantage.

"That's a whole different affair. Jacob left me no choice, you see." He drew closer, stalking her, closing in until only inches separated them. She could feel his anger, rising off him like heat from the blacktop. The hatred in his eyes cut through her. "When I told him Melissa had caught on and was forcing my hand, *he* decided to come out of the closet. *He* decided to reveal the secret, without thinking it wasn't in *my* best interests. One scandal would have crucified me and ruined my political career. Do you think I planned to stop at mayor of this Podunk town?"

"I can't believe Jacob loved you," she snarled.

Matt paused, sucking in breath through tight lips, then laughed. "Yes, Jacob was different from me. He was willing to give up everything just to tell you and Abe the truth before someone else did." His eyes unfocused. He looked away, seeming to see another time, another place. "When I realized he planned on divulging the secret against my will, I freaked. I tampered with his brakes and, with the help of Mother Nature's downpour, created a very nasty, wholly believable accident."

Anger seared through her, clean and white, blinding her to all but one thing. He had killed Jacob and nearly destroyed Abe's life. "I hope you burn in hell," she hissed, and lunged.

He stumbled back, surprise flashing across his face. She thrust her knee up and hit him solidly in the groin. Grasping his crotch, moaning, he fell to one knee. Pain twisted his face.

"I'm not stupid, either," she said, and bolted, but he shot a hand out and caught her ankle. She jerked free, kicking at his twitching fingers. Dee dashed for the front door and grappled with the bolt with trembling fingers. Finally she twisted it and tried for the chain lock.

"I don't think so, you bitch," Matt whispered from behind her.

She turned and flattened herself against the door, breathing hard. He stood leaning against the counter, still gripping his crotch.

She backed away, but he flung himself at her. Before she could do more than turn, his hand snaked into her hair. Pain iced through her scalp as he hauled her back, fingers tangled in her hair like a fly in a spider web.

He threw her onto the floor. Her knees hit hard and she fell forward, landing on her hands. Something snapped in her right wrist with a dull *crunch*; she hardly felt the pain through the hard shock of adrenaline. Rolling quickly, she kicked out at him, trying for another groin shot. Instead she struck his left knee. Howling, clutching his leg, he tumbled to the floor. She rolled to her feet, staggering.

He growled and popped up off the floor. "Bitch!" he snarled through gritted teeth. The veins around his eyes popped. "Enough. I'm done playing with you!" He slammed into her, forcing her back to the floor. Her head struck the wood. Pain exploded behind her eyes, darkened her vision and knocked the breath from her lungs. Before she could suck in another his hands closed around her throat, fingers digging in, squeezing the life from her.

She clawed at his hands, nails raking furrows, but he held fast, his greater weight and strength bearing down on her. Black edged her vision. Her lips worked fruitlessly, struggling for breaths that wouldn't come.

Desperate, she grabbed at his head and pushed her thumbs into his eyes. He screamed, flinging his head back, but she held on tight even when his grip on her throat strengthened, crushing down. She choked on a sound, but dug her thumbs in deeper until he screamed again, let go and grabbed at his face.

The moment the chokehold released, she twisted free, kicking back from him. He swore at her, grabbing for her blindly, but she rolled onto her hands and knees, reeled to her feet and made a break for the bedroom. His footsteps hounded her, relentless on her trail. She ducked into the bedroom and swung around to close the door but he thrust his bulk into the doorframe, blocking it.

"Stay away from me!" she screamed, and shoved him. He grinned, his eyes red and wet.

"Not on your life," he said, and struck her hard across the face. She slammed into the floor. A red cloud of pain closed over her, slowly turning black as her vision dimmed.

The last thing she saw was his patent leather shoes, coming closer and closer.

Chapter 18

As Abe pulled out of town and onto the highway, a terrible anxiety weighed his heart. Dee. Why was he worried about her? He hadn't thought it possible to obsess over a woman as he'd obsessed over her. The last time he'd come even remotely close had been in junior high, too long ago to even matter.

He'd almost told Dee where he was going today, but he'd wanted it to be a surprise. Let her think he was running errands. She didn't need to know he'd gone to the jewelry store afterward. Nor did she need to know about the engagement ring in its little velvet box.

These were modern times, he knew. Many women wanted to pick out their own ring, but Abe was a traditionalist. If Dee's father were around, Abe would ask for her hand. His mother had told him stories of how his father came to her house and asked for her hand in marriage. They'd lived happily ever after, 'til death did they part.

That's what he wanted with Dee. Happiness and eternity. In his heart, he swore they would have it.

Abe knew without a sliver of doubt that he loved Dee, had loved her for many years. His mother had warned him that one day a woman would come along and turn his world upside down. Never would he have thought it might be his brother's ex- fiancée.

The last few days had made him realize he needed to be with Dee, to love her, marry her, father her children. The mere thought of their future children brought a liquid warmth to his chest.

Abe punched in her number on his cell. No answer.

He sighed. Why wasn't she answering? He tried Mitch. His voice greeting came over the line. Abe's heartbeat accelerated. Mitch always answered his phone. Something was wrong. He knew it to the marrow of his bones.

He had to do something. He punched in Sheriff Stansey's number. "Sheriff Stansey here..."

"Hey, Don--" The phone went dead. He looked at the screen and cursed. No service.

Abe drove frantically. Within fifteen minutes he careened up the driveway, braked in a shower of gravel and jumped out. He'd barely opened the door when he heard a scuffle upstairs.

"Dee?" he yelled as he raced up the stairs. He heard her scream, then all went quiet.

As he crested the stairs, the sight before him chilled his heart yet ignited his blood with a fury he'd never known. Dee laid motionless on the floor, sprawled in the doorway of her room. Matt stood over her, fists balled.

"What the--"

Matt jerked and turned, eyes wide. Abe leaped forward; Matt threw his hands up, but Abe's greater bulk knocked him back against the wall. Matt struck hard and reeled back, swaying. Righting himself, he took a swing at Abe and struck his jaw.

Abe barely felt the blow. Rage drove him, gave him strength, and he slammed his fists into Matt's face with a satisfying *crunch*. Matt buckled and Abe struck him again, over and over, until Matt fell, groaning, to his knees. Abe kicked him in the stomach, the head, the back. He might have killed him if not for a gurgling sound from Dee.

She was alive! He raced to her and fell to his knees at her side. Blood trickled from her nose, her cheek showed signs of bruising and her shirt was ripped. Her eyes fluttered and she moaned as he gently laid her head in his lap.

"I'm here, sweetheart. I'm here now."

Dee's eyes fluttered open. As she looked up at him, tears spilled onto her cheeks. "Abe, it's Matt." Her words were husky.

"He's out like a light," he assured her. "You're going to be fine." Some of the rigidness left his body.

Dee screamed, "Watch out!"

Abe turned and caught a glimpse of a vase as it came toward his face. The next thing he knew he heard a bone-jarring crash. A sharp sting cut across his temple. Through blurred vision he saw Matt standing above him.

The light faded as he fell to the floor.

* * * *

Dee sat up woozily and fumbled to her knees at Abe's side. Blood poured from his right temple. "No! Abe, oh God, Abe." Tears flooded her eyes and seemed to drown her breaking heart. He lay still, so still, the man she loved sprawled in a puddle of his own blood.

From the corner of her eye, she saw Matt reach into his pocket and take out something shiny. As she turned, he snapped open the knife's long blade. "I didn't want to do this. I don't enjoy killing." He shook visibly. His eyes were wild. "It's all your fault, you know. If you'd just left town, none of this would have happened. You've ruined everything."

"I didn't ruin anything, you lunatic!" she screamed. "*You* killed Jacob. You did! He cared for you!" *Don't provoke him,* caution warned. She ignored it.

"You lousy bitch! Things went south when you seduced Jacob in Hawaii. Don't you get it?" He laughed harshly. "His plan was perfectly maneuvered. He was going to go away, find a Little Red Riding Hood to bring home to his big bad wolf of a brother. He flew to an island and caught the first dumb whore he could find. I'll take blame for that. I talked him into the wife. It's a cozy set-up and I thought he'd be happy. You were so stupid. Wasn't it obvious he wasn't attracted to you?" His laughter grew bitter. "He told me he tried to make love to you, but he couldn't do it."

"The only thing he couldn't bear was his guilt. He wasn't deceitful. He learned that from you. You've betrayed your wife and children. I guess it's not so hard to make love to her, is it? What is it, pity? Or do you get off on screwing decent people over?"

He sighed heavily. "I did love Alexis at one time, and I tried to deny my feelings for Jacob. I've loved him since high school. A man of my caliber is expected to have a wife, children and the white picket fence. I have that life, and I've worked hard for it."

"So now what? You've killed the man you love and hurt countless people. Stop now, for your kids," she pleaded.

In her peripheral vision, Abe's hand twitched. Panic clutched her. If Matt realized Abe was alive, he'd finish the job and Dee wouldn't be able to stop him. She stood slowly, making sure Matt's eyes were on her as she stepped away from Abe, and hoped desperately she remembered everything from her self-defense class.

"Think about it, Matt. No one knows you played a part in Jacob's accident, and I'll keep it a secret. You know I can keep secrets. I kept Jacob's secret even when I could have told Abe. Walk away now, and everything will be okay. I'll leave town immediately, and you can go back to the ways things were."

Matt's hand lowered slightly, fingers going lax on the knife. He craned his head, his cruel scowl easing only to be replaced by a cold smile. "It's too late." He thrust the knife toward her. "Now do as I say, and I may let your boyfriend live. I may even let both your boyfriends live." She gasped. He smirked, twirling the knife. "Mitch isn't dead, but I can easily remedy that."

"Mitch has nothing to do with this. He's nothing to me."

"You could have fooled me. After that kiss at the barn, I wasn't sure who you liked more, Abe or the hick."

Her mouth dropped open. He continued, "I thought I did such a good thing when I told Abe you'd left upset. It worked like a charm when he went in search of his poor girl-toy. I thought he'd force you to leave, seeing you in Mitch's arms. Then you'd run away like before and my problem would be solved. No such luck." He shook his head. "Now, are you ready to do what I ask?" He stepped closer.

She nodded. The tip of the knife penetrated her thin shirt and cut her skin as he held it against her back with an unsteady hand. "Go down the stairs," he said. "Slowly. Remember, I'm watching you."

Obediently, she took the stairs one slow step at a time. If she pulled away at the bottom, could she run fast enough to escape? His hand on her shoulder and the knife at her back warned her not to try. As if he read her mind, he pushed the knife deeper. She winced and tried not to scream. One hard thrust and he could bury it in her flesh and kill her. She held her breath, counted, exhaled as her relaxation exercises had taught her. Calm. She came to the foot of the stairs and let him shove her toward the door. She had to stay calm.

Or that bastard would kill Abe and Mitch.

Outside on the porch, Matt paused and scanned the drive. "Where are the keys to the Jeep?" he demanded.

"I don't know."

The knife dug deeper. "Care to change your answer?"

She pointed back into the house. "On the table."

"Are you lying?" he snarled.

She shook her head rapidly.

"Damn."

They backtracked slowly. When he saw the keys, exactly where she'd said they were, he said, "Very good." He grabbed them. They headed back outside. He handled her roughly, half pushing, half dragging her to the Jeep, swearing as he unlocked the driver's side door.

He slid across the driver's seat into the passenger side, pulling her behind him until she sat behind the wheel. The entire time he kept his grip firm, the knife digging into her side.

"Where are we going?" She tried to keep her voice steady, but it trembled. If they left the farm, her chances of survival dropped from slim to almost none. Could she signal for help? Hadn't she dropped her cellphone on the floor? Maybe Matt hadn't seen it. It was still open; she might have a chance.

"I know a quiet little place on the outskirts of town," he said gleefully. "It just so happens they're pouring the concrete for a building tomorrow. I bet they'd never find a body buried in cement."

"You'll never get away with this," she said. She shifted in the seat, pretending to squirm away from the knife to mask what she was really doing: slipping her sandal off and using her toes to feel for the phone. If she could find the redial button, she might be able to reach Melissa in time to save three lives.

"Why not?" He bent his face to her ear and ran the backs of his knuckles down her cheek. When she jumped, he narrowed his eyes and laughed.

If the worm of a man got any closer, she wouldn't be able to maneuver the phone without getting caught. If he figured out what she was doing, it was all over. There would be no second chance.

Dee began to sweat. She needed to keep him talking. "You don't really want to do this." Her foot cramped. She couldn't concentrate with his heavy breaths in her ear, the knife biting into her side and her toes crawling over a phone. She found the redial button only by dint of the large keys. They'd saved her from her clumsy thumbs many times. Now, they might save her life. "I know you feel like you're up against the wall. We've all felt that way."

"You don't know how I feel." His lips caressed her ear. She shuddered. "You are pretty, you know. I appreciate that. Alexis is pretty, too."

"I thought you liked men." She tried to keep her voice steady.

"I like beautiful things, no matter what." His breathing grew rapid, shallow. "I bet Abe fucked you good. Better than he did that slut Melissa." He pressed his nose to her hair and inhaled. She flinched. "Your fear is strong. I smell it. It's...alluring." His other hand fell to her thigh. "I want you. But you know that. I wanted you the moment Jacob said he'd marry you--just because I knew I could have you."

He jabbed the knife against her side. She hissed through her teeth. She could feel blood hot against her side, sticking to her shirt. "Maybe I'll show how much you want me," he said.

She pushed the button. He jerked. She braced for the blow, certain he'd heard the beep. Yet he glanced outside, craning his head to peer through the side window.

"What the--"

A loud *bang* came from the back of the Jeep. He jumped, the knife hand dropping. Dee took her chance and shoved the door open, flinging her weight against it with such force she tumbled from the Jeep. Her shoulder hit the gravel hard and she skidded. A stabbing pain in her ankle jerked her back. Her foot was stuck in the door hinge. She lay there a moment, gasping and dazed. The sound of Matt's cursing spurred her to move. She heard him scrambling across the seat toward her.

She pulled and tugged on her ankle, but it wouldn't budge. Where was Matt? He should have been on her by now.

She risked a quick glance over her shoulder, first left, then right. Hauling herself up, she peered into the Jeep. It was empty. When another wary glance proved she was alone, she focused her attention on slowly maneuvering her foot free. Wincing as it popped out of the door, she crawled to her feet. Standing hurt, but she forgot the pain as she heard two bodies thudding and scraping against the gravel.

She limped around the car, her head throbbing and her body aching. Near the front fender, Abe and Matt rolled, locked in battle with fists flailing. She grabbed at the hood of the car to steady herself as the blood drained from her face. Abe rolled, shoving Matt beneath him, and struck him hard across the jaw. Matt's head fell to the ground, hitting with a shallow *thud*. His eyes rolled back as, with a groan, he passed out.

Abe turned to her. His face was pale, and dried blood covered one cheek. "He better hope he stays out." His voice was rough.

She limped to him and wrapped her arms around his neck. "Are you okay?"

He rubbed his brow, just below the wound, and squinted. "A little sore, but I'll be okay." He held her at arm's length and looked her over. "Are you hurt?"

"Bruised and scared, but I think I'm okay."

The sound of a siren burst into the quiet night. "Who called?" he asked.

"I owe Melissa a beer. I'll explain later."

"Damn, you're bleeding." He gently lifted her into his arms and set her on the passenger seat of the Jeep. He began checking her for injuries.

"You came to my rescue," she whispered. She kissed his cheek. "I owe you a beer, too."

"A beer?" He smiled.

Rhonda Lee Carver

He lifted her shirt. His gentle fingers examined something on her side. She looked down and saw the long cut on her skin. He said nothing, but the panic in his eyes said it all.

"There's more, but I'll save it for later." She ran her hand down his cheek. Exhaustion, fear and pain finally ate at the adrenaline rush, leaving her weak and dizzy. Abe swam before her eyes, became two Abes, three, then one again. She needed to lie down.

A battered police car came slewing into the drive, spraying gravel. Before it even braked fully, Sheriff Stansey shot from the driver's side and hurried toward them. He looked over Abe's shoulder. In Dee's vision he was only a blur of color, the radio in his hand a blot of black that wavered as he raised it to his mouth "We need an ambulance out here at the Delaney Farm, as fast as they can get them wheels rollin'."

"Hi, Sheriff Stansey." Dee gave him a smile. She started to feel a little sick to her stomach.

"You two look like hell." The Sheriff took off his hat and held it tightly against his chest. He glanced down at Matt's motionless body and asked, "He dead?"

"I wish." Abe muttered. He didn't take his gaze from Dee. She smiled. "Hang in there, baby. We got an ambulance coming."

Sheriff Stansey bent and checked Matt's pulse. "You're right. He's still alive." The knife Matt had used was next to his still body, stained in blood. The sheriff kicked it to the side and brought out his cuffs, snapping them around Matt's wrists. "I doubt he'll give us much of a fight, but putting this scum in cuffs feels damn good. I never liked the son of-a bitch myself." A low moan came from Matt, but he didn't move. "You have the right to remain silent..."

Sheriff Stansey's voice faded. Dee reached up and laid her hand on Abe's shoulder, squeezing. "You have to find Mitch. Matt did something to him," she whispered.

Everything went dark. Sheriff Stansey's voice chased her into the blackness. "It's going to be one long night."

* * * *

Dee woke in the hospital, her arm hooked to an IV, her wrist bandaged and her ankle wrapped. Abe sat in the chair at her bedside, slumped over at the waist. His head, wrapped in white bandage and gauze, leaned precariously against his fist.

"Abe?" she whispered. Her throat was dry and hurt like fire.

He jerked, then came fully awake. His eyes widened. "You're awake."

"Yes." Her jaw ached.

"Hey, baby." He kissed her cheek.

"How did I get here?" She glanced around the white, sterile room.

"It's okay. You've been in the hospital for almost six hours. The doc kept you sedated while they did some testing. You're fine, minus a few bumps and bruises and a broken wrist." He kissed her forehead. "The cut on your side needed stitches. But it wasn't too deep." His eyes misted. "And the baby is fine, too."

"Baby?" Had she heard right?

"The virus wasn't a virus at all. Doc ran a precautionary test before he filled you with meds. He said you're early enough that the symptoms could have been mistaken for illness. You didn't know?"

She shook her head and a pain ripped through her head. "No." She lowered her hand to her stomach. "I...I...but we used protection...except for--"

"The time in the barn."

"And by the pond. Neither one of us was thinking. Are you disappointed, Abe?"

"Not in the slightest. Lie still and save your energy. Everything is fine. We'll talk about the baby when you're better. You got some stitches in your side, where the knife had cut you. It'll be a story you can tell our grandchildren some day."

"What about you?" She reached up and lightly touched his cheek. "You had a nasty cut."

He shook his head. "Sweetheart, it was nothing." He kissed her chin, then the other cheek.

"Is Mitch okay?" She swallowed the fear in her throat.

Abe pulled back just enough to look into her eyes. "Matt had come up behind him in the barn and struck him over the head, tied him up and left him in the corner. Besides a bruised ego and a desperate need to kick Matt's ass, he's fine. He's out in the waiting room with Melissa."

"That should be an interesting conversation," Dee said.

He smiled. "It'll make time pass for them."

Alexis came to mind. Her stomach churned. Poor Alexis. "We have a lot to take care of. I'll have to talk with Alexis..."

"She knows everything. Sheriff Stansey went to her house right after he threw Matt into jail. I guess she was pretty shaken."

"The kids...she must be devastated."

"Sweetheart, she's safer now that Matt is out of her life. He was bound to flip. He could have hurt her and the children next." He swept back a tendril of her hair. "Matt's in jail, and we have all the proof we need that he caused Jacob's death."

"You know?" Dee bit back the tears that misted her eyes.

He sighed. "I do. Right now, no more talk of that son of a bitch. Only you and how you're gonna get better. I love you, Dee."

"Come again?"

He chuckled. "It amazes me that after what you've been through, you can still joke around." You have a question to answer. And you know what question I'm referring to. Or should I ask again? Let me rephrase that..." He stood, retrieved his jacket and drew something from the pocket. When he returned he sat on the edge of the bed, took her hand into his and asked, "Will you marry me, my love?"

He opened the velvet box. Nestled inside was the loveliest princess-cut diamond she had ever seen. The jewel twinkled in the light.

"Did you say you love me?"

"If you don't know that by now, you should. I am madly, completely, insanely in love with you, Dee. I want nothing more than to call you my wife, to spend the rest of my life with you and to raise our children together."

The tears fell to her cheeks. "Abe, I thought I'd never hear you say those words."

"I'm an ass, remember? Like all asses it takes us a little longer to get the job done, but when we do we get it done right." He touched her cheek. His hands were worn and weathered, yet his touched warmed her body to her soul. She could look into his eyes and see his eternal love for her. She wanted to live her life in his embrace.

"Yes. Yes, I'll marry you. I love you. I never stopped loving you, no matter how much I tried, or what came between us. There's nothing holding us back now. I want us to be together, to grow old as man and wife."

And they did.

Epilogue

Dee pulled out the last pie, fanning herself. She'd been going nonstop in the diner's kitchen all morning, and needed a breather. She pulled the bun at her nape loose and finger-combed her hair. After serious renovation and redecoration, Dee reopened the diner under a new name, *Hope's*. Business had been booming since.

"Is this all twenty pies for the Detty party? Abby's here to pick up the order."

She turned to Alexis. After Matt's life sentencing, Alexis had come to work at the diner and start her life over. "Ten apple and ten blueberry." Dee glanced over the stacks of boxed pies. "Ready to go." She grabbed one pile, and Alexis took the other.

When Dee pushed through the swinging door, Abby met her with a smile. "Thank you, Dee. I know it was short notice for such a huge order. I owe you free piano lessons." Abby beamed.

"I'll hold you to that," Dee said.

The bell above the glass door dinged and Dee's heart skipped a beat, as it always did when she saw her husband and daughter. Abe held Hope in the crook of his arm. The little girl had her face buried in his shoulder. "Hello, my love." Abe kissed Dee, pausing to look into her eyes before pulling back.

After over a year of marriage, Dee couldn't believe how their love continued to grow. How could it be possible? Dee patted Hope's back. "What's wrong with my butterfly?"

At the sound of her mother's voice, six-month-old Hope pushed herself up from Abe's chest. A cherubic smile spread across her toothless mouth. "Ma." She lifted chubby arms out to Dee.

"Come here, sweet girl." Dee lifted her daughter into her arms for a warm hug. Dee inhaled her soft baby powder scent.

"She must have missed Mommy," Abe said.

"I didn't expect to see you two so early." And she must look a mess after her busy morning.

"I've come to steal my wife away. Mom has agreed to watch Hope while I get my woman all to myself. You know Mom wants to spend time with her granddaughter before she heads back to Florida next week. "

"I...I don't know if I can get away." Dee glanced over her shoulder at Alexis.

"Go, Dee." Alexis winked. "I'll take care of things. Mrs. Graves is here, plus I have Mitch coming in later to help."

"Oh, that's not help, Alexis," Dee teased. "You know Mitch isn't coming in for the daily special--at least, not the menu special."

Alexis' mouth dropped open. "You be good, Dee Delaney. You know Mitch and I are just friends."

Dee laughed. "If you say so." She turned to Abe and slid her fingers down his chest. "I guess I'm all yours."

He grinned. "A man has never been happier."

Dee looked from her husband to Hope and back to Abe. Joy made her skin tingle. "And no woman has ever been happier."

She'd realized it wasn't a house or a farm that made a home. It was the people she loved, those who loved her. It was in the heart.

Dee was home.

Meet the Author

Suffering from years of hopeless romantic notions and sexy, sassy heroines and bad-ass heroes taking up residence in her mind, Rhonda decided to write and bring the stories to life. With baby on hip and laptop on the other--and two years later--Rhonda has published five eBooks with a handful of spicy love stories waiting for the final touches. When Rhonda isn't crafting edge-of-your-seat, sizzling-ink novels, you will find her with her children, watching soccer, watching a breathtaking movie, doing (or trying) yoga, and finding new ways to keep her smile bright. Rhonda thrives on making her readers happy. She believes everyone deserves romance--one page at a time...

Rhonda's Website:
www.rhondaleecarver.com
Reader eMail:
Rhondaleecarver.author@gmail.com

Turn the page for a special excerpt of Rhonda Lee Carver's

Dreaming Ivy

Can a past love become their future?

The Thorntons' mansion is full of timeless secrets waiting to be unraveled. When small-town journalist Ivy and ghost hunter Max are stuck in the forgottena, dilapidated house, they find more than just a haunting. Ivy finds herself dreaming of the former owners, Marcus Thornton and his lovely wife, Elizabeth. Their profound love was once the talk of the town, and the cause their mysterious, untimely deaths never found. When Ivy's dreams begin to become reality, the mystery starts to unravel and sheds truth on more than just the past.

WARNING: Graphic language, naughty ghosts, a non-committal male, and a love that endures beyond time and death.

On sale now!

Chapter 1

"I must be hearing things. I've lost my mind. Or have you lost yours?" Ivy Kennedy eyed her boss, Marshall Deatrick, across the stretch of his paper-scattered desk. Her blood pressure rocketed. Sweat beaded between her breasts and on her upper lip. The air conditioning in the historical downtown building was on the fritz again. Tugging at the neckline of her blouse, she uncrossed her legs. "I could quit, you know." She swallowed back the bitter taste of reality. She knew it was a weightless threat.

"Well," he began easily, "you could quit, but we both know you won't." His lips parted with smug satisfaction. He lifted the lid from the antique box on the corner of his desk and took out a discount cigar. He laid his large frame back into his shabby leather chair as if he were relaxing into a bubble bath. He slid the cigar under his nose, taking a long, slow sniff like it was premium tobacco.

Ivy counted to ten. Her patience wore thin. "I hope you're not planning to light that while I'm here. The heat and your arrogance are all that I can endure at one time." The rotating fan on his desk squeaked as it turned, blowing hot air into her face. She pressed her fingertips to her temples.

"Don't push it, Ivy."

Dropping her hands into her lap, she sighed. Marshall was an intimidating man, but she'd learned over the years just how far to push. "Why this assignment, Marshall? Why stick me with a ghost hunter? You know I don't believe in ghosts and paranormal activity. It's amazing what people will write about to earn a buck."

He rolled the stogy between his fingers, then placed the cigar into his front pocket and patted it like a loved one. "Now, now, Ivy. There's no reason to get your panties in a bunch."

"That's a sexist remark," she snapped.

"Forgive me. Don't get your boxers in a bunch. Better?" He started to reach into his pocket but caught himself. Ivy knew he'd been making a sizeable effort to stop smoking. It was putting him on edge, obvious by the tense set of his jaw and deeper lines around his eyes.

"Much better." She rolled her eyes. It was no use. Marshall didn't understand the concept of political correctness or treating people with respect.

"There are a handful of columnists and reporters in that room--" He flicked his thumb toward the outer offices. "--that would give their eyeteeth to grab this story."

"Oh really? Let's take a look at the handful jumping for this opportunity." She swiveled in the chair. She looked through the dirty window into the work area. Five desks filled the space, separated by short, gray dividers. One desk was occupied, not unusual for a Sunday afternoon. Jimmy Doyle, fresh from college with a golden journalism degree, had joined the Morgan Tribune two months earlier. The wet-behind-the-ears kid left a lasting impression of being an ass-kisser. She had nothing against the guy. In fact, she liked him. She respected anyone who had drive and passion matching her own. Too bad the ladder of success only had two steps above them. To get a better position at the Tribune, one would need to pry dead fingers off the rung.

She turned back to Marshall. He'd claw the eyes out of any person who dared to overstep him.

"Why not give this story to Jimmy? You don't see anyone else hanging out here on a Sunday, do you?"

"You are," he said.

She ignored his comment. She was always there. "Jimmy would get a kick out of staying in a haunted house for two weeks."

Marshall shook his head and scratched the top of his shiny, bald head. "Don't try it. It won't work."

"Try what?" She lifted a brow in dispute.

"To push this story off onto someone else. It's yours. Like it or not."

"Why me?" She shivered. Her voice was close to a whine. She didn't like to bellyache but there were moments. She considered herself a true journalist, open to all stories, but there came a time when she had to stand up for what she believed in. This was where she drew the line. "I've been here for five years, Marshall. Aren't I supposed to be above and beyond all of this small-time news? Hasn't my column doubled in readers in the last two years? Don't you like my articles? Isn't that worth something?"

"You want big? Go about two hundred miles upstate and you'll get your massacre headliners and your TV highlights. Here, you'll get what is available." He shrugged when she groaned. Maybe a silent apology?

"Look Ivy, you're my best journalist. I realize you think you've earned the right to call the shots, but you're not looking at the whole picture." He scooted forward in his chair. "For example, about that story you did last week. You know, the one about the stolen lawn ornaments. The day after the story ran, the thief was caught, thanks to your amateur detective work."

Why did his comment feel more like a slam than a pat on the back? He said it like it was something grand. It wasn't a prized moment for her. "Marshall." She leaned forward too. "The thief was a ninety-six-year-old escapee from the convalescent home. He had been suffering delusional outbreaks and thought he was a savior to all statues of the world. When he was busted, the deputy couldn't tell who was moving faster: the ornament or the thief. It wasn't a big-deal story and it didn't take a genius to figure out the culprit wasn't a clever thief with a devious, complex plan. The sheriff's office just didn't want to waste time on a pointless crime."

Marshall got up from his chair. He moved his large frame around the massive cherrywood desk and propped himself on the corner like it was his throne. "What do you expect, Ivy? Old men stealing lawn ornaments are the story here. If anything, you gave people a laugh. We're running a newspaper for a town of less than thirty thousand people, not a city with a population of drug users, felons and murderers. A tale like Thornton House with its ghost sightings and so-called haunting is news to these townsfolk. It has been the curse and talk of these parts since before you were the twinkle in your mother's eye. For an admired ghost hunter to come here from Chicago to investigate...Well, that is a huge story." He sighed. "I don't get why you're dragging your heels on this."

Ivy had a murderous urge to look Marshall straight in the eye and tell him where to shove this so-called story. With great control, she swallowed her pride. As much as she hated to admit it, and would refuse to say it aloud, he was right. Bigger stories than a ghost hunter coming to town wouldn't be on the horizon. "I'm curious why this ghost hunter thinks it's a value of his time and effort to come all the way out here to investigate paranormal activity. The house hasn't been lived in for years. Is he really in that dire need of snapshots of ghosts and goblins? You'd think they would have enough horror stories in Chicago."

"Tsk, tsk, Ivy." He clicked his tongue. "You're becoming cynical with age. Your hunger is growing into an evil beast."

At least she had hunger. "I'm just pointing out the facts."

"And you're saying you don't believe Thornton House is haunted?" One bushy brow popped up.

"We both know the story. I did a piece on the house and its history when I first started working here, remember? There were so many rumors swirling around town. My intention was to piece the puzzle together." She sat back. "People have lost sight of what's real and what's fantasy. They've glorified the house with stories of murder and mayhem. There is history there, but--"

"History of a rich landowner who died a lonely man," he interrupted. "A lot of people believe the spirit of Marcus Thornton and his wife still roam the halls of that old house. Others believe he buried his fortune somewhere on that property." Out of pure habit, he took out his cigar and took a few unlit drags.

"If that were true we'd have the whole town over there digging up the property. Now that would be a story." She laughed.

He shrugged. "Maybe it's time someone found a truth to all those rumors. And that's where you come into the picture."

"I've already been there and done that. There is no truth to the rumors. It's pure drama that keeps the rumor mill turning."

"But this will be different. You'll be there getting first glance."

"Why is this so important to you?" No doubt he had an ulterior motive. He always did.

"Imagine the publicity it will bring to our little town. We have to be a part of this, Ivy. We can't just let some out-of-towner come in and grab our story. We gotta get our piece of the pie. Not to mention that Mayor Tisdell and the owner of the Tribune, Mr. Parks, are breathing down my neck for me to make this work. Since they got wind of this man's arrival, Tisdell and Parks have been fired up, twisting and spanking this opportunity half past dead. We've kept it under wraps until the definite plans were made."

"All over a ghost hunter?"

"This ghost hunter's investigations are well known in his field and gobbled up by believers--and some not-so-believing. He's written a shitload of books on his observations and findings. They sell like crack hotcakes. Imagine all the tourists who'd want to come here just to get a glance at that old dump." His eyes sparkled dollar signs. "However, if my plan works..." He stopped.

She saw the mischief bubbling in his chubby face. "What are you up to, Marshall?" She narrowed her eyes. "Who is this man anyway?"

"Max Shepard. Heard of him?"

"Maybe, but once again, paranormal activity isn't my cup of tea." And then a thought struck her. "Wait... Isn't he the man who was in all the gossip magazines after he divorced that paper-thin supermodel? She walked the catwalk for those fancy fashion designers. When was that--maybe five, six years ago?"

"I don't know about all that nonsense." He snorted. "You know how those good-for-nothing tabloids feed off the crud of other peoples' lives."

"You mean the same sort of trash magazines you worked for before coming here?"

He didn't even acknowledge that. "Why he has chosen to come here and investigate the dilapidated Thornton House makes no sense to me." He rubbed his palms together. "What I do know is that Shepard made arrangements to stay at the old dump. The latest owner of that shack is all for this investigation. He sees this as a future sale in the making."

"You mean your golf buddy. Nice how that fits so comfy. Let me guess--you scratch his back, he'll scratch yours?"

"I have a lot of golf buddies, sugar."

"And what makes you think this ghost hunter guru would want some writer tagging along? Aren't most of those people loners?"

His eminent sneaky grin returned. "I'm afraid that choice won't be given to him. The property owner arranged for you to stay also. It's all been smoothed out. No worries. Just do your job."

"That's nice," she muttered. "Okay, let's say this man is worth a story. But what a waste of time investigating Thornton House for haunting. There's nothing to find but cobwebs and rats. I'd rather just skip the whole haunting buzz and go straight for a personal interview with Max Shepard." She grinned. "I bet I'd get a good one."

"Thatta girl." He stood up and straightened his tie. "And you never know, Ivy. From the photos I've seen of Shepard, he's a looker and known as a ladies' man. You may have to use those womanly wiles to convince him to give you an exclusive. Cozying up to him might be a blessing instead of a disaster." He winked.

"Oh…my…my…my." She surveyed him closely and her stomach twisted. "What are you thinking? You wouldn't! You couldn't!" she sputtered.

"What, Ivy?" He pretended innocence, which was a long shot. "Just remember us when you get that interview."

"I've never used seduction to get a story, Marshall. I won't start now."

He rubbed his double chin and shrugged a beefy shoulder. "That thought never crossed my mind. But just between the two of us, sex is not taboo in getting an exclusive. You could do worse things--"

Ivy jumped up from the chair, sending it hard against the wall. "Stop right there. There is no chance in hell I'd lower my values for a story. I will not go in there and seduce this man to convince him to let us publish his personal story. This is deplorable."

"Calm down, Ivy. I'm not asking you to seduce the man, for Christ's sake. I'm just asking you to go in and get a story on what he finds. Show Shepard how nice our townsfolk are. If he gives you an exclusive, that'll be icing on the cake. Look at it as a partnership. And being the journalist you are, think of the story you can get from him. And what if he picks up on a few freaking mysteries and ghosts? If we earn a story in one of his books, well hell, this town will no longer be stories of stolen lawn ornaments. Can you only imagine the boost such a story can give to a writer's career?" He pointed a stubby forefinger in her direction.

Ivy didn't respond. She toyed with the idea of an exclusive on Max Shepard. She didn't care whether there were spirits or walking dead. What she did believe in was finding an opportunity to make a name for herself. A story on *the* Max Shepard would be of interest to a lot of people, and definitely wouldn't hurt her lackluster career. "I think this Max Shepard is a phony. He claims to see ghosts? I bet he's never seen a spark of supernatural his entire life. Now that would be a story. To reveal a fake."

"A fake? Sure, go that route. I don't give a rat's ass what your storyline is as long as there is one. Find out what makes this man tick. Stay on him like white on rice."

"Desperate, are we?" Ivy raised a brow.

"When you get to be my age you'll know desperation." Something flashed across his face. Ivy couldn't read what it was before it disappeared. Was there more to this than met the eye? He turned toward the window and stared out. "Besides, you're a journalist. Journalists like to report. Maybe this is the story that'll get you that move into a big-shot newspaper. If not, you may be stuck in this small town for the rest of your life. Unless we both fail on this story and get fired."

She sucked in a deep breath. "That sounds like a threat."

"Well, one way or another, you may get your wish." He turned back to her. "You'll be leaving dodge by choice or involuntarily." He chuckled but it didn't quite reach his eyes. He returned to his chair.

"Marshall, you know I came back here to live for one reason and one reason only. My mother and her ill health. She needs me. I need this job until I have a backup plan." With her dismal thoughts burning a hole in her head, she told Marshall, "You should be glad that I'm still here doing your demeaning jobs. I bet we wouldn't see your star reporter, Jasmine, sleeping in a deserted haunted house for two weeks."

His scoff echoed off the empty walls. "You're a much better writer than Jasmine. Good looks, big tits and a tight ass can only get you so far in life." He thrummed his fat fingers on the desktop.

"And what am I? Chopped liver?" She scowled.

His face softened slightly. "Ivy, you don't need me to feed your ego. You're single because you choose that life. You've got the whole kit and caboodle. Looks, brain and future."

"I'll remind you of those sentiments later. And if I get this story and those photos, if he takes any, I better land a huge raise and a private office, you hear?"

"Does this mean I can count on you?" He was already smiling in success.

"On one condition. Well, two conditions." She smiled.